P9-ELR-928

The Letter Writer

OTHER NOVELS BY ANN RINALDI

Juliet's Moon

The Ever-After Bird

Come Juneteenth

An Unlikely Friendship
A Novel of Mary Todd Lincoln and Elizabeth Keckley

Brooklyn Rose

Or Give Me Death
A Novel of Patrick Henry's Family

The Staircase

The Coffin Quilt
The Feud between the Hatfields and the McCoys

Cast Two Shadows
The American Revolution in the South

An Acquaintance with Darkness

Hang a Thousand Trees with Ribbons
The Story of Phillis Wheatley

Keep Smiling Through

The Secret of Sarah Revere

Finishing Becca
A Story about Peggy Shippen and Benedict Arnold

The Fifth of March
A Story of the Boston Massacre

A Break with Charity
A Story about the Salem Witch Trials

A Ride into Morning
The Story of Tempe Wick

ANN RINALDI

The Letter Writer

A Novel

HARCOURT, INC.

Orlando   Austin   New York   San Diego   London

Requests for permission to make copies of any part
of the work should be submitted online at www.harcourt.com/contact
or mailed to the following address: Permissions Department,
Houghton Mifflin Harcourt Publishing Company,
6277 Sea Harbor Drive, Orlando, Florida 32887-6777.

www.HarcourtBooks.com

Library of Congress Cataloging-in-Publication Data
Rinaldi, Ann.
The letter writer/Ann Rinaldi.
p.   cm.
Summary: A young girl who serves as letter writer for her blind
stepmother is haunted by her unwitting role in Nat Turner's rebellion,
one of the bloodiest slave uprisings in the history of America.
1. Southampton Insurrection, 1831—Juvenile fiction.   [1. Southampton
Insurrection, 1831—Fiction.   2. Turner, Nat, 1800?–1831—Fiction.
3. Slavery—Fiction.   4. African Americans—Fiction.   5. Virginia—History—
1775–1865—Fiction.]   I. Title.
PZ7.R459Le   2008
[Fic]—dc22   2008009283
ISBN 978-0-15-206402-0

Text set in Adobe Garamond
Designed by Cathy Riggs

First edition
A C E G H F D B

Printed in the United States of America

To Karen Grove, my editor
at Harcourt for over fifteen years now.
With thanks for all your help and patience.
There should be more like you.

Prologue

He came to me when I was just eleven, Richard White-head did, and asked me to be his mother's letter writer.

"Her eyesight is failing, you know," he said of her. "Within a year she won't be able to write her letters anymore."

I knew, for I was with her every day. It was my job to know such things. It had, in a household where every-one more or less had a "job," fallen to me to be her com-panion when I wasn't at my lessons. I had reported her failing eyesight to *him* a while back.

"Mother Whitehead bumped into a chair today, Richard. She may have hurt her knee." Or: "She mis-placed her notebook, and we spent the morning looking for it, and when we found it, she had to bring it up to her nose to read it, Richard."

But I had to be careful how I said these things. He had a deep and abiding love for his mother. She was not my mother, you see. We both had the same father, dead now, but different mothers. Though I loved Mother Whitehead as my own.

Besides, Richard was the eldest, and, at twenty-six, unofficial head of the family. And if all that was not bad enough, he was a Methodist minister and, as such, was not above making me kneel on the gravel on the back drive for an hour if it pleased him.

And on many occasions, if something was gnawing at his innards, like weevils in the cotton, it could please him. Not only with me, but with my "girl" Violet and even betimes Margaret, his beloved sister whom he so spoiled.

That gravel was hellish on one's knees.

When he asked me to be Mother Whitehead's letter writer, he'd had the doctor over to examine her and decided plans must be made.

"Her correspondence means the world to her," he said to me. "She writes voluminous letters."

"But I'm only eleven years old," I protested.

In Virginia, in the year 1830, eleven is considered almost a young lady. You are expected to behave as such. No more tree climbing, no more sliding down the banister, no more playing with dolls, although I line mine up on my bed pillows each morning and still address them by name. Oh, one can still play the game of Lame Chicken or put on men's clothes in disguise at a party, but for the most part one is considered grown-up at eleven.

"You won't need to start this writing for about three months, according to the doctor," Richard told me, "and anyway I've seen your penmanship and it is, by far, better than any eleven-year-old's that I've seen. Pleasant has done a good job with you."

Pleasant, his wife, was my personal tutor.

"What you can do," he suggested, "is start corresponding with someone for the next few months. Improve your writing even more."

But with whom? He thought a moment while he rifled through the mail that had been set down on his desk. Then he looked as if he had a brilliant thought and took up an envelope of cream-colored paper that looked as if it had traveled through several continents. He scowled at it. "How about this fellow? Writes to me regularly, asking about the crops, the animals, and other matters about the plantation. He's our father's brother."

"Mother Whitehead says he's touched in the head."

"You must understand she was estranged from our father before he died. By the time he had you with your mother in London, things were finished between them. The only reason they weren't divorced then was because he knew it would destroy her social status. The last time she saw him was when he made that visit and left you here. I think it was kind of her to take you in, being that you were the child of another woman and visible proof of his infidelity. Don't you?"

I felt my face go hot. "Yes," I said. And to myself I added, *And you never let me forget it.*

Whether this was the cause, or it was just the nature of our beings, Richard and I were often estranged from each other. The only closeness we had was when he talked about "our father." And when he talked I kept a still tongue in my head and listened, because in spite of his overall meanness, he was the only one who ever explained the hopeless entanglements of my family to me.

He cleared his throat. "Uncle Andrew has been hinting lately at being invited here for a visit," he said. "So I must admit I have a twofold purpose in asking you to write to him. One, to improve your writing and learning. The man is highly educated. And two, to hold him off on visiting. It would put Mother into shock to see him again. Bring back too many sordid memories. I must protect her."

I nodded yes, said I'd do it.

He was pleased. It didn't take much to please Richard. Just do as he said, with blind loyalty. Like my older sister, Margaret, did. I longed to be able to be like Margaret. If she were a cat she'd be rubbing against his legs. I couldn't be like that, and so I was always in trouble with him.

But oh, to think he at least respected me for my dignity. To think if I only had that.

For the next three months I corresponded with Uncle Andrew and got to know him. Or so I thought.

One

*D*ear Uncle Andrew: My name is Harriet, and depending on how much you can abide my chatter, I am going to be writing to you a great deal over the next year or so. My brother, Richard, demands it, and when he demands something, the angels concur. He says you are a very intelligent man, and though Mother Whitehead says you are touched in the head, you suffer that malignancy no more than most of us in this family. At any rate, he says you are also an art dealer. And the engraving we have in our center hallway of Mary Wollstonecraft was given to Mother Whitehead by you many years ago. Good grief, I have *been passing by it for years! I am eleven years old, love to ride horses and read books. My best friend is my "girl" Violet, who somehow came to be half white and almost part of the family. I don't know how, but this family is so confused it is like Mother Whitehead's crochet yarn after Piddles, the cat, gets finished fussing with it. Oh, I must go now, they are calling me for Sunday dinner, and if there is anything Richard hates it is one being late for prayers before meals.*

Your servant, Harriet Whitehead

Violet was at the edge of the pond in water up to her knees, cutting the cattails. "Oh, look at this one, Miss Harriet," and she snipped it off expertly with a scissor. "This one's a beauty." Her skirt was hitched up between her legs showing her light brown thighs. She didn't wear ruffled pantalets like I did. Slaves didn't wear pantalets.

I took the cattail in my hands with the three others. It *was* a good one. I could cut a sharp point and it would prove to make a good pen when dipped in some lamp-black. I'd use it to write my next letter, I decided. Maybe this afternoon.

Neither of us paid mind to the rider approaching on the fat white horse until he was nearly on top of us.

"What are you doing there in that pond?" Richard demanded. "Getting cattails again? Violet, get out and put down your skirts. Harriet, give over those cattails."

He reached out his hand. I gave them over.

"Going to use these for writing, are you?" he asked.

"Yes," I answered.

"They're known around as slave pens," he said. "Look on the back of any barn wall and you'll see their scratchings. Or messages, made from cattails and lampblack. You know what lampblack does to your clothing, Harriet. And how Mama hates it. Yet you do persist. Why?"

"They're more of a challenge to use," I answered.

He sighed deeply. "Haven't you enough challenges in life? Violet, haven't you anything better to do with your time?"

"It be the Sabbath, Massa Richard. I done went to church. An' if'n I must say so, you did preach a fine sermon, yessuh." She used the special voice she always used with my brother, the subservient one with the humble tone.

ANN RINALDI

"Such a fine sermon that you come home and raise your skirts in front of everybody, hey? You're not a child anymore. How old are you now, Violet?"

She was untwisting her skirt and pulling it down. "Fourteen, suh."

"That's right, I keep forgetting. You're three years older than Harriet. Well, you keep acting like that and it'll be time to marry you off."

"But suh, I be Miss Harriet's girl. I been carin' for her since she come to us. And I serve Miss Margaret, too, when she come home from that fancy school in Jerusalem. An' I run and fetch for your mama. They all can't do without me."

She was begging. And pompous Richard let her beg.

"At any rate, my sister has letters to write this afternoon. And not with cattails. So you go about your business, whatever it is. And if I catch you with your skirts hiked up again, they won't come down until I've given your legs ten stripes. You hear?"

"Yessuh." Violet ran.

I looked at him. "You know Mother Whitehead doesn't hold with having her slaves mistreated."

"You're scolding *me* now? Since when do I report to you?"

"That isn't it."

"What is it, then? How does Mama think I keep order around here? Somebody has to put the fear of God into them. Tell me, can you recollect the message of my sermon this morning? Or would you rather spend an hour kneeling on the gravel in the drive?"

I thought desperately. Something about servants. Yes. Oh yes. "Slaves, obey your masters," I said.

He looked disappointed.

"Mother Whitehead wants you to keep order," I said bravely, "but she also wants you to do right by them."

His face got red, not a good sign. Still, he controlled himself. "Now you go on," he said with quiet dignity, "and look in on Mama. She's on the front veranda. See if she needs anything. And the less you have to do with Violet, the better off you'll be. Slaves have no morals. I mean it, Harriet. I can forbid her from being around you if you think I'm fooling."

"I know you're not fooling. You never fool. You have no sense of humor."

He glared at me. I knew he was warring inside between his man-of-the-cloth instincts and his basic brotherly anger, and it tore at his innards. Because I was the only one who caused him such conflict.

I really believe that I was the only one in the family who made him, on occasion, sorry that he had become a minister. I squared my shoulders and walked away.

❧

I always wished I could be as accomplished as my almost-mother, Catharine Whitehead, blind as she was. I wished I could be mistress of a plantation like Whitehead Farms, respected by all, copied in dress and style of living, mistress of sixty negroes, living in a white-pillared house, with a dead husband who owned a fleet of ships.

And all those apples on the ground out there, piled up under the trees and ignored while everyone complained about being poor because the Virginia soil was worn-out from hundreds of years of tobacco growing. (Not us, thank God, we had the income from Father's shipping business.) And all the while the apples were falling down and hitting people on their heads, until they finally woke up from their tobacco dreams and said "cripes" or whatever it is that one says when God Himself strikes you.

"Cripes, what are we complaining about? We've got apples to make into brandy." And so in all those barns of all those plantations appeared stills to convert the apples into applejack.

'Twas the apples that brought us prosperity again. I say "us" because there's no use in having money if those around you don't have it.

And it was the apples that brought us Nat Turner. But I get ahead of myself.

Mention Nat Turner and I must make mention of my sister by half, Margaret. You see, we don't do anything in wholes in this house, though we pretend to. Looking at Margaret, older than me by four years, you know she's nobody's half, but her own whole self. Beautiful and composed and hitting you on the head with her presence when she walks into a room. And she is only fifteen.

Margaret is out to torture Nat Turner. And there he is again, creeping into the conversation, just like he crept into our lives, loaned to us when everyone got on their feet after the business with the apples. Loaned to us from Mr. Travis, his master, to make furniture for the front parlor. He is good at making furniture.

Margaret treats him like this whole family treats darkies. She won't give him a second glance, though she taunts him by swishing her skirt when he passes, by dropping her handkerchief, then bending over to pick it up, only he retrieves it first for her and she thanks him and stays bent over so he can get a good look at her bosoms from her low-cut dress.

I've confronted her about it. "You can't do that with negroes," I told her, "like you can with white men."

"Why?" she asked. "Because they aren't in charge of their senses?"

"No, because if he's caught looking at you later, or smiling at you, he can be whipped. And Richard will have it done. It isn't fair."

Margaret isn't one for fairness.

But here I am, Harriet Whitehead, eleven years of age, only half belonging to them, half of me a part of them and half I don't know what. Nobody has ever told me about that half. My father, Mr. Whitehead, Richard and Margaret's father, and Mother Whitehead's late husband, is dead, lost at sea on one of his many vessels.

Perhaps he would have told me about the other half had he lived long enough.

Why is he called "the late Mr. Whitehead," I used to wonder. I know now. Because it is too late for him to tell me from whence I come. Too late for him to help Mother Whitehead by writing her letters for her to her business associates. Too late for him to tell Margaret to cover her bosoms, and too late to tell Richard to let up on me and stop making me kneel and pray for my sins.

So I take refuge in making up from whence I come. At night I lie in bed and do it. One night my mother might be a princess from India. My father's ships went there, didn't they? Another night she is closely related to British royalty, and so on.

If it is on a day when I have written a letter to Malta for Mother Whitehead, I just know my mother came from there.

You see, this job that has fallen to me to do, I don't mind doing. It is something that awards me a sense of dignity. Because I know all Mother Whitehead's personal and business activities. She writes to almost everyone in Southampton County. She is friends with people in important places. She can tell you who is going to have a child, whose marriage is not going well, who has a terrible sickness, and whose son was put out of Harvard for bad behavior.

There is no one who wouldn't do her a favor.

The week of Christmas last year, Mr. Fitzpatrick, the local drunk, came knocking on the back door. Richard wanted to put him out, but Mother Whitehead insisted he be let in. He begged her for some money. He had four children and no money to buy them presents. Mother Whitehead gave him a sermon about drinking. He promised he would stop, though both he and she knew he wouldn't.

She gave him some money. He promised he would repay it, though both he and she knew he wouldn't. And he left, bowing and kissing her hand.

That is the way Mother Whitehead is regarded. I'd like to be regarded that way, too, someday. I'd help people, but I'd give a scolding first.

I'd scold Richard good, if I had the chance. Then I'd let him kiss my hand.

If that isn't power, I don't know what is.

Two

I do not recollect much of when I first came here. There was a green baby chair, I recall, that was mine. One day I was put in the kitchen in it, away from the family in the dining room because I was not "behaving" and I was mad beyond anything I can remember. There was the stairway I wanted to climb but was forbidden to, and the marvel of the Christmas tree the day my father brought me home to this plantation in Virginia when I was just past two.

He set me down on the Persian carpet in the parlor in front of everyone.

"This is Harriet," he said.

The tree they had was all prettified, with packages under it. Oh, I'd seen Christmas trees in London far more beautiful in my short life, but this tree stood out because it was decorated with popcorn and someone had cut out a chain of small white angels to go round it. Trees were new in the colonies in 1821, but Christmas was greatly celebrated in the South. The tree dripped with goodies, candy, and cookies; a child's delight. I ran to it.

Someone caught me up just before I got there and pulled me close to his tweed jacket. It was a young man who I later learned was Richard, on his Christmas break home from Hampden-Sydney College, already studying to be a minister.

My father had packages, too, gifts he'd brought, and he handed me over like I was one of them. I just stared at everyone. I stood there on my fat, two-year-old legs, my feet in my black laced-up shoes digging into the carpet. I had tolerable good sense in those days, just as I have now. So I didn't cry. I just stared.

I must say they gave me a welcome that was not exactly as warm as it was curious. That is to say, they fussed over me because I was Papa's "foreign get," as Richard put it. Years later I found out that it meant I was Mr. Whitehead's child from a foreign wife and not the lovely

Mother Whitehead, who sat like a queen in her chair in the parlor, overlooking the scene before her.

I was passed around and greatly exclaimed over. The Whiteheads also had another little girl whose name was Margaret, but she was already six and making her demands known. I was soon toddling after Margaret. We played at dolls, at all kinds of games. Without knowing it, I even accommodated her by not being as beautiful as she was, and that seemed to endear me to everyone in the house. Margaret knew it, too, and never let me forget it.

She knew she was superior to me. It showed in little things. For some reason, when the dressmaker came, she'd get the brightest fabric. She'd get silk while I got cotton. As we got older, she even managed to get Mother Whitehead to agree to low-cut gowns. I wouldn't dare ask for such.

The only one privy to these little hurts was Violet. And she would buoy me up in such times by saying things like: "Don't you let it worry you one bit. Your face has more character than hers, anyway." Violet was "given" to me and Margaret to be our own private "girl." To fetch and carry, to help us dress, and to pick up after us.

Margaret slapped her on occasion. I never did. Light-skinned Violet, with her blue eyes, became a favorite of mine.

I liked her better than Margaret, who soon proved herself a ten-karat pain, insufferable in her demands about dress, quickly bored and always boring, short on imagination and long on dullness, quick to demand compliments and slow to give them. Her one talent was playing the piano. She took lessons at Miss Dangerfield's School for Young Ladies in Jerusalem.

Margaret boarded there all week, which gave us a recess from her. But she came home on weekends with her nose in the air because she was a "private school" girl, and therefore ordained better than us by holy decree.

I soon hated her. And she, me.

Weekends, when she came home, I was always in trouble. Richard was out of the seminary by now and making a good stipend as pastor of the local Methodist church.

My father had left after that Christmas visit when he brought me to stay, promising to come back, but breaking his promise by going off to sea in one of his ships and getting himself killed before I was three.

Things were tenuous enough for me, at best. Mother Whitehead became my guardian, she who had endured the humiliation of having her husband's child by another woman in her home. She took it on herself to raise me.

And she did it with a sense of fairness, justice, and compassion, as she conducted all her affairs.

I ought to know. I write her letters.

Dear Mr. Copley: Yesterday your three cows broke through the fence in my upper five acres and ate a good portion of my corn. I was raising that corn special for the Southampton County Fair and it was superior in texture and substance and consistency. However, us being neighbors for so many years, and your cows being superior in texture and substance and consistency, I am willing to let the matter go. One does not demand payment from a neighbor. Anyway, the fence needed mending, and I neglected it, so the fault is mine as much as yours.

Your neighbor, Mrs. Catharine Whitehead

In spite of his duties as a minister, Richard took over as head of the family. He dealt with the overseer, set the rhythm of work on the plantation, disciplined the slaves and us children. Sometimes, with the exception of Margaret, I think we children, Violet and I, fell into the same category as the slaves.

There were times it seemed like Mother Whitehead was oblivious of what Richard was doing. But she knew. She always knew. And she let him go only so far before she stopped him.

He married Pleasant and they moved in with us. Pleasant had been a schoolteacher before marriage and was now appointed my personal tutor. She lived up to her name.

Seven years went by. In that time, when Richard was not aware of it, Pleasant privately tutored Violet, too. Knowing Richard would not approve, Pleasant and I kept it a secret. Having a secret with someone creates a bond between you, and soon Pleasant and I were closer than real sisters.

We shared all kinds of thoughts. I often wondered how my brother, Richard, so stern and tied up inside his head, could win the love of someone like Pleasant. But somehow she kept his edges smooth. God knows what he would have been if not for her.

In those seven years, Pleasant got with child twice. One was stillborn and the other a miscarriage.

When I was nine, Pleasant was brought to bed with a baby boy. They named him William, and he is the darlingest baby boy that God ever made, and we all love him.

⌒⌒⌒

I think that School for Young Ladies that Margaret goes to in Jerusalem is a witches' den. She is supposed to be "finished" there.

Well, she has done a few samplers, she can make Richard a shirt with the most exquisite stitching, she can work a quilt, she can make candied violets and pour tea and make small talk to fill the silences at a gathering, when all I can do is sit there like a jackass in the rain.

And she can handle the negroes on the place. She has this way of talking *at* them, not *to* them. And, at age fifteen, she gets them to "yes, Miss Margaret" her and curtsy to her as they leave the room.

I will never know how to order them around. They call me just Harriet. And some of the older ones tell me to sit up straight at the table. And Ormond, our man-about-the-house, who sometimes waits on the table, often has to take my linen napkin out of my hands and stand over me and spread it on my lap. Not one word passes his lips. Not one. He just does this and then moves away.

While across the table, Margaret smirks at me.

Richard not only orders the darkies around, he has them whipped. How he, a man of the cloth who mouths pious phrases in church on Sunday, can oversee the whippings of innocent human beings, both men and women, infuriates and puzzles me.

He will order other darkies to watch.

You can hear the screams all over the plantation.

One particular Sunday I had locked myself in the library with Papa's books, where it was dark and safe, where the blinds were drawn against the summer sunshine and I felt close to my father, who would never countenance such doings as having the negroes whipped.

Mother Whitehead was on the side veranda, which was covered with clematis that cast shadows like angels' wings, sipping one of her cool drinks.

The brass knob of the library door twisted, then the door opened. "Here you are."

It was Margaret, all done up in white with a blue sash, for it was Sunday. Richard never put off whippings because it was Sunday, and he'd preached an especially fiery sermon that morning, which gave him the courage to match his own convictions.

"Aren't you going to come out and see the demonstration?" Margaret asked.

I was poring over a copy of *Romeo and Juliet*. I looked up, horrified. "You were watching?"

"From a distance, yes. Richard wouldn't let me get close. Oh, he deserved that whipping, that evil Henry."

"But he's just a boy!"

"Man enough to peer down my dress when he helped me from the carriage after church this morning. I told Richard." She twirled and inspected herself in a mirror. "Oh, yes, I did. And he's being punished with fifty lashes even now."

"Well, then I'm going to tell Richard that you enticed Henry on purpose. That you always entice the negroes." I got up. The book clattered to the floor.

She laughed. "Do you think he'll believe you? I'm his favorite. You know that. He'll do just about anything for me. Anyway, he's not going to sell himself short in front of the other darkies by calling it off now. They have to learn, and guilty or not, they have to learn here and now." She grabbed the brass knob of the door and turned before leaving. "Aren't you supposed to be attending my mother?"

"Connie is doing that."

"Connie is out witnessing the demonstration. At Richard's orders. You know Mama sees only forms and shapes. You'd best get to her or I'll tell Richard. Then you'll get fifty lashes' worth of words." She laughed again, started out the door, and again paused.

"Is it true that Mother offered Mr. Travis a premium amount of money to hire Nat Turner to work for us?"

I was almost afraid to answer. "I don't know."

"Liar. You write the letters. What did she offer? Do you know that Turner considers himself a minister? Can you imagine? How would you like him baptizing you?"

"He is said to be a genius with furniture making," I told her. "He learned when he was about sixteen. He was apprenticed out. And you know how Mother wants new tables for the parlor and the hallway."

She just stood there. "So Mother did ask for him."

"I'm not supposed to talk about any of her private correspondence," I said.

"Well, she'd best be careful. He can read and write. One of his previous masters taught him in an experiment. And now nobody knows quite what to do with him! So Mr. Travis hires him out and uses the money he brings in."

"Well, that's one thing to do with him, I suppose," I said.

"Well, what would you do, Miss Holier-than-thou? You think you're so all-count better than the rest of us because you sympathize with the darkies. Well, you think Richard doesn't?"

"I can hear, right now, how he does," I said.

"Well somebody has to keep them in line or they'd kill us all in our beds at night. You think Richard enjoys doing it? But he knows he has to. He's a minister, for heaven's sake. A man of God. He knows his earthly re-sponsibilities, taking care of us. You think he hasn't con-sidered what's to become of the slaves in Virginia, even before you put foot on the place? You think Mother, sitting out there on the veranda, isn't thinking of it right now?"

I sighed. "If I'm wrong, I'm sorry," I said. "But I just don't think this is the way."

"If you come up with a better one, let us know. And go on now to Mother." She went out the door, leaving me alone in the room.

Nat Turner. I had heard of him even before Mother wrote asking to hire him. I had heard Turner was a fa-natical minister, a man who went about telling people he'd seen visions in his dreams, who baptized people in ponds. How could he take orders from Richard, who believed ponds were only for fishing in? And if he had a vision in his dreams, would he wake up and tell his wife it was because he'd had too many fresh oysters for supper?

I sighed again, sensing trouble, and went to see to Mother Whitehead.

Three

"Would you like any more lemonade, Mother White-head?" I came upon her on the veranda, just where I'd left her, only now her head was back against the flowered cushion and she was dozing. The piercing blue eyes opened. "I want dinner. When is dinner?"

"Connie said in half an hour."

"What are we having? I'm about starved. Where is Violet? Why isn't she fanning me? Where is Owen? I need these wicker shades pulled down."

"Owen ran off, Mother. Two weeks ago now. Don't you remember?"

The negro boy in question was fifteen. She'd raised him up since he was two. He was the son of Jack and

Charlotte, who'd been with her forever, as had most of her people. Of a sudden Owen had felt the call of being free, and one day a couple of weeks ago he simply could not be found anywhere.

Richard was furious. Because Mother wanted Owen back so badly, he'd spent forty dollars already on travel expenses, meals, newspaper ads, and rewards trying to find the boy.

NOTICE FOR A NEGRO BOY NAMED OWEN.
Source: The Richmond Constitutional Whig.
Runaway from the subscriber living near Jerusalem in Southampton County. June 2, 1831, a negro boy age 15, five feet two inches high, slim, well built, active, and likely, wears his hair in two plaits, smokes segars when he thinks nobody is watching, and walks with considerable confidence when he thinks people are. He can cook eggs, make coffee, wait the table, answer the door, fetch and carry, and do all other houseboy duties with admirable grace. Wearing a cotton shirt and pantaloons and good homemade shoes when he ran. May be headed for the Canadian border. Fifteen

dollars in gold coin will be rewarded the finder for
giving over the above-described negro.
      Mrs. Catharine Whitehead
      Owner of Whitehead Farms
      Southampton County, Virginia

It must appear in the *Richmond Whig*. No other paper would do. Richard was furious because his mother made him take the buggy on the fifteen-mile trip across the Sussex County line to the Sussex County Courthouse, where Evans and Blanding, the slave auctioneers, did their business. She made him watch at the pen where negroes were likely auctioned off, to make sure Owen hadn't been already captured and wasn't being resold again into bondage for four hundred and sixty dollars, or some other outrageous sum.

Violet told me she knew where Owen was. I believed that she did. Food was missing from the pantry. Exactly the kind of food that could be spirited out in a napkin or cabbage leaves without making a mess. Sometimes when I was about the place, I had the feeling that Owen was about, too. Watching us. Here all the time and laughing at us.

"I want another drink," Mother said. "And I want liquor in it. No sissy-boots lemonade. And I don't want Richard to know it." She handed me the glass and I took it into the house, to the sideboard in the dining room where the liquor was kept, and mixed her a mint julep, exactly as she liked it. She drank. I couldn't blame her. If I were husbandless with a plantation and sixty slaves to worry about and a son like Richard and a dizzy daughter like Margaret who went to an expensive girls' school and learned nothing, I'd drink, too.

I brought the glass out to her and she accepted it. "We have time for one letter before dinner," she said.

I set myself up at the small ladies' desk next to her. It could be moved from room to room by a servant, and it held her fancy stationery and all her accoutrements for writing.

She dictated a letter to her dressmaker in Jerusalem.

Dear Mrs. Ord: I hope this finds you and yours in the best of health. In answer to your last question, I have decided that for my new gown I shall need at least twenty-five yards of fabric. I would like it to be of violet taffeta, trimmed with bias bands of black velvet edged with white at the bottom of the skirt. I will

*likely be able to make a fitting by the end of June and
will require this gown for the Fall Festival in honor
of the success of the crops to be held in Jerusalem in
September. Keep in mind that while made of taffeta, it
must be elegant and genteel. As for my daughters, we
will discuss their dresses when I come for my fitting.*

*Thank you, Mrs. Catharine Whitehead
P.S. Oh, by now you must have heard that my
houseboy, Owen, has run off. We think it is just a
prank, but he is missed terribly by all, and I ask you to
please send around a courier if you have seen him.*

I felt guilty not telling her what I heard. But Violet
had begged me not to. And I kept my promise.

Then she said that since there was still time we would
do one more letter. This one was to Mr. Travis, four miles
down the road, and the theme was familiar.

*I wish you would have a change of heart about hiring
out to me your darky, Nat Turner. I have heard he is a
first-rate worker, that he can read and write, and does
not need someone standing over him all the time
telling him what to do, that he has invented a privy
flusher, the kind that would be fed by water from my*

33

windmill. I need a barn designed for my prize cattle, some good oak furniture fixed, and many an honest day's work done around here for which I would pay premium prices.

She had been trying to "acquire" Nat Turner now for six weeks. But Mr. Travis had refused to hire him out. "What do I have to do?" she asked me. "Offer to buy him?"

Not until that afternoon did I have time to write the letter I wanted to write. It was to Uncle Andrew.

Uncle Andrew brought me into a world I'd never known. He told me about his friend John Constable, the landscape painter, who had studied at the Royal Academy Schools and was recognized as the foremost landscape painter in Britain. I learned all about Constable, the way he painted, what he painted, and how his wife died.

I made my mind up that I would travel to England someday. I would go to the Lake District, where all the great artists and writers seemed to go.

I had, without realizing it, another tutor in Uncle Andrew.

He knew Joseph Cottle, too, the British bookseller, who was a patron of Coleridge and Wordsworth. He sent me a copy of *Lyrical Ballads*. And Margaret became so jealous she just had to take it to school and show it around. I prayed she wouldn't lose or destroy it somehow, for it had Coleridge's signature inside it.

Margaret told everyone it was hers.

I learned a lot about Uncle Andrew. Mostly I learned that we felt the same about slavery, God, and family. My family knew I wrote to him and did not object, so long as I did not speak of him. He was, for some reason no one would name, the black sheep of the family.

That day I wrote and told him about Owen.

Likely he is hiding out in the thick, swampy woods that adjoin our property. Slaves all flee there when they run away. Some run away regularly when they want to be treated better, then in good time they come home. The slaves at home will bring them food.

I know that slavery in England ended in 1807. I suspect you people in England think we are barbarians at best for still following the practice. Well, Owen has been gone near three weeks now. I wonder if Violet is feeding him. I might let her take me to see him. Or then again, Uncle Andrew, I just might bring him some food, myself.

Four

*D*ear Mr. Peyton: I have been informed by some of our neighbors that you are fortunate enough to have produced turnips for sale and turnips to spare. If this is true, I would like to purchase 10 or 15 bushels. Let me know the price. This year we have sowed only our freshest land in turnips since we presumed that wearied lands would not bring them. They were used as food for Whites and Negroes and also for cattle and sheep. Mr. Young told me he planted turnips to be fed on only by sheep and as the basis of the improvement of poor lands. We will try that experiment here this year, only with buckwheat . . .

For two hours I had written letters concerning the improvement of land, the rotating of crops, and what fertilizer was best. By the time we were finished I knew that turnips as well as hemp and pumpkins were best planted on new clearings of land. And that eight acres of pumpkins, well grown, will feed all the stock we have for two to three months. Those letters taught me more than I learned from Pleasant about my geography and numbers together.

～

It was to be a warm June evening, turning into the kind of night when you didn't want to go to sleep but stay up all night talking.

I asked Mother Whitehead if I could sleep upstairs with Violet. "I see nothing amiss with it," she said.

I made her an eggnog with rum in it, her favorite bedtime drink, and left her there in the parlor. She would have her "talk" with Richard before she retired. They talked every evening, and mostly it was about the running of the plantation.

We sat on Violet's bed, inside the mosquito netting, and I felt like a girl in a fairy tale. "Tell me about Nat Turner," I said.

"Did Mother Whitehead get his master to lend him out yet?" she asked.

"She wrote him another letter," I told her. "But I don't know whether we'll be getting him. Violet, do you know where Owen is?"

She giggled. "Well, he isn't here, so stop looking around. But I do know where he is, yes. He's with Nat Turner."

I'd known, as a matter of course, that she was a follower of Nat Turner. All negroes who considered themselves of any eminence around the Southampton area of Virginia were. But I'd never asked her about it. I'd never intruded on her privacy.

The sound of a night bird drifted in the open window. A single tallow candle gave a flickering light. "Why is he with Nat Turner?" I asked. "And where are they?"

"Nat heard he'd run off and went to Nelson's Pond, where he'd been told he was hiding. It fits right in with Turner's plans. He's going to do a baptism there tomorrow."

The pond was at the abandoned Nelson plantation. The property must have been beautiful when once lived in, with that spacious pond in front. Now it seemed haunted. The owners had fled when people were fleeing these parts and going south because the soil could no longer support their tobacco growing.

"Have you ever seen him do a baptism before?"

"A few times."

"What's it like?"

"Have you ever seen your brother do one?"

"Yes, but it can't be like that, because Turner has no church."

"Tomorrow, he's baptizing old Ezra Bentley. Well," she elaborated, "he takes the person right into the water, then dunks them under and holds them there for a minute while he says the words."

"Ohhh," I breathed, "how dramatic."

"Yes." She nodded with self-importance. Then she leaned close and whispered in my ear. "Ezra was chased out of your brother's church for being a drunk and a gambler. He wanted baptism, but your brother said no."

I nodded solemnly.

"I always thought people who were sinners were supposed to go to church," she reasoned. "And not be thrown out. But it seems that Richard wants only the ones who aren't sinners."

I nodded, agreeing.

"There's more." She smiled triumphantly. "Owen's

going to be at the baptism. Yes"—she nodded her head vigorously—"he is. He wants to come home, you see. But he's afeared of what Richard will do to him. So he's gone to Nat Turner and hopes Nat will speak with Richard as one minister to another and talk Richard into not whipping him for running away."

"Ohhh," I breathed.

"So if you want to come, we go tomorrow."

"Are we going to bring Owen some food?" I asked.

"Yes. I've got it all arranged with Connie in the kitchen. She's going to make some egg salad sandwiches and wrap them in cabbage leaves. For Owen and Nat."

I felt envious that she could call Nat Turner by his first name. But she seemed perfectly at ease with it.

"We'd better get to sleep now," she told me, "or we'll both get in trouble before we even do anything."

I was just about bursting to tell someone I was going to one of Nat Turner's baptisms. Of course, to me, Nat Turner was part real and part fancy. Isn't that the way he was to everyone in Southampton County? I'd heard rumors and I'd heard fact. He was a nigra minister who'd had visions. He was a slave who'd invented a privy flusher, flushed by water. He was a preacher who held

Bible class for his own kind, and he could repair an oak table better than a trained furniture maker.

You could die to meet him and at the same time you were frightened beyond belief at meeting him. He was a slave, sold and resold, hired out at premium prices. Mother Whitehead wanted him but couldn't get him. Oh, I wanted to tell someone I was going to see him do a baptism. So I wrote inside my head:

Dear Uncle Andrew: Tomorrow is Sunday and I am going with Violet to watch Nat Turner do a baptism. I am so excited. You know who Violet is. And I've written to you before about Nat Turner. He is a real renegade in these parts, like your Robin Hood. Don't worry for me. Violet and I are going to bring Owen home! I hope all is well with you.

Your loving niece, Harriet Whitehead

Five

⁂

Before breakfast the next morning, which was Sunday, Mother Whitehead was up and about and insisted on dictating a schedule to me to be posted on the wall inside the large barn.

It was a plan for the year of the planting and harvesting, and it even told how many horses and oxen and laborers were to be used.

> *Calendar of work for 5 laborers, 2 horses, 4 oxen, 3 great and 3 small ploughs on a farm of 6 fields of 40 acres each, hiring aid in harvest and hay time.*
> *Sept. 1 thru 17—plough in the stubble of the first wheat field and sow buckwheat, 40 acres in 13*

*ploughing days. Sept. 18 thru Oct. 1—plough and
sow wheat after clover, 40 acres in 13 days with 3
double ploughs . . .*

And on it went: when to haul corn, firewood, coal,
wood, rails, when to deliver wheat. It was Mother Whitehead's yearly calendar of work. I found it fascinating. She
said I was to make two copies and put one on Richard's
desk.

Richard was put out with her for working on the Sabbath, but she told him that this was God's work as well
as was his sermon writing. What, she asked him, could be
more God's work than planning on sowing the wheat in
the fields?

Richard had no answer for that so he couldn't argue.

At breakfast Violet served and was careful not to look
at me. I moved my eggs and bacon around on my plate
but none of it reached my mouth.

"She isn't eating, Mother," Richard complained.
"She's planning some mischief. Look at the appetite Margaret has."

Margaret did some simpering thing at him, which
pleased him enormously. I gave a look of disgust. Margaret had his approval, and I knew that I'd rather have

Richard's rage than his approval. To have his approval would mean that I'd failed in life.

I forced myself to eat, lest he make Mother drudge up some ungodly chore for me to do this morning. Richard went back to reading the *Richmond Constitutional Whig* newspaper. He'd been up since six, going over his sermon, and until he gave that sermon he was not to be borne.

"Leave her be, Richard," Pleasant said. He sat at the head of the table and she on his right. The baby, two-year-old William, sat between them. He was playing with his egg, shoving it into his mouth with his fingers. "Da, Da." He waved a spoon at Richard.

I loved William. And Pleasant. With the exception of Mother Whitehead, whose presence always brought peace, they were the only light touch we had in the house, because they melted your heart. Pleasant with her beautiful light brown hair around her shoulders and William toddling around getting into everything. They were the only ones who could soften Richard up. William, with his fat little legs and dimpled face, could toddle over to his father and mellow all the meanness. I know now why God gave us babies. They required constant attention, of course. They made messes and disturbed the peace, but their cuteness and smiles were sometimes the only reminder of God we had in the house.

And Pleasant had the privilege that a loved wife had. She was the only one who could scold Richard, make him mind, point out the error of his ways. I loved her, because without her we might all consider ourselves in hell.

She came from a family of eminence in Petersburg. She was well schooled and had tutored wealthy girls before marriage. I respected her, for many reasons, but mostly because she could handle my brother.

Soon it was time to go. Mother Whitehead knew where we were off to, and Richard had reluctantly given permission after breakfast, which meant I would miss his church services. He gave permission only because he, himself, wanted to know what a baptism of Nat Turner's would be like and he, of course, could not, because of his position, attend.

I excused myself and left the room. But he followed me out into the hall. "Be respectful," he admonished. "I don't know where this outrider of a minister was ordained, but it's still a baptism. You hear me?"

"Yes," I said.

He looked at Violet. "You hear?"

"Yes sir, Massa Richard."

"You riding?" he asked me.

I said yes.

"Give Violet a horse. Blackie. William could ride him, he's so docile."

I said yes to everything and he went back to the dining room. We went to the kitchen, where we collected our food, then out to the barn where Chancy the groom readied our horses.

When we got to the pond where the baptism was to take place, we were surprised to see it surrounded by at least seventy-five poor whites and negro people, come to see Nat Turner the minister, just as we had come. Word had traveled, as it does in these parts, on some grapevine that never stopped growing and could never be cut.

"There he is," Violet pointed out. "There's Nat Turner, with Ezra Bentley."

I looked to where she pointed. And sure enough there was a tall, young negro man with short hair, broad of shoulder, and dressed in trousers that were torn at the knee and a shirt that needed buttons in front. Immediately I saw that there was something about him that drew the eye and the mind. But I could not say what.

Without stopping, he grasped Ezra Bentley's arm and together they walked right into the pond in water up to their shoulders. Then, of a sudden, Nat Turner grasped Ezra by the shoulders and pushed him under the water. While he held him there with one hand, he recited something from the Bible, something long enough that I thought Ezra might drown. Then he shouted, "I baptize you, in the name of the Father, and the Son, and the Holy Spirit, amen."

Ezra came up like a hooked fish, sputtering and choking and yelling at the same time. "I am saved! Thank the Lord God, I am saved!"

No sooner had he shouted that than some white boys from the shore splashed into the water, all of one mind, and waded over to Ezra and grabbed him and pushed him again under water.

"Stop it." Nat Turner reached under to rescue Ezra. "Hear me! How dare you interfere with a sacred ceremony!"

But they were not afraid of him. They did not consider him a true minister. I thought of my brother and how those boys would cower if he spoke to them in such a tone. These boys hooted at Nat Turner. They splashed water at him. And when they finally let poor Ezra up out of the water, they shoved him at Nat and the two of them

ANN RINALDI

fell and went under again. The boys left, calling Nat names as they went.

It was then that I noticed a lone figure on the shore, pacing up and down.

"There's Owen," Violet said to me. And she waved him over.

He came, head down, eyes casting around, like one who was hunted and did not want to be found.

"How are you today, Owen?" Violet asked.

"I'm all right, Violet. Why did you bring Harriet?"

"Is that any way to greet someone who cares about you?" Violet asked.

"Hello, Owen," I said.

He nodded at me. At home he'd often spoken to me. His job had been to keep the many hearth fires burning in the house, to clean the chimneys when they needed it. And Mother Whitehead had been training him up to answer the door when someone knocked.

He was even learning to send the person around to the back door if they were negro or looked disreputable.

"Are you coming home today?" I asked him.

"No. I'm not comin' 'til Nat Turner brings me."

There was a surprise. I hadn't known Nat Turner was coming to our house. Violet grabbed me by the arm then, and pulled me over to where Turner was standing, wiping himself down with a dry piece of flannel. "Nat," she said, "this is Harriet Whitehead. I want you should meet her. She's one of the Whitehead daughters."

He stopped rubbing his head with the towel and gave a little bow. "Pleased, Miss Harriet," he said. His English was perfect. His yellow brown eyes took my measure.

"I've heard a lot about you, Mr. Turner," I said.

He laughed then, a not unpleasant sound. "Mr. Turner? You do me an honor. I can't remember ever being called Mr. before."

"Should I call you Reverend?"

"You should call me Nat, like everybody else does. Unless they're calling me 'boy.' Or 'you there.' Or something worse. You saw the crowd. Nobody thinks I'm a reverend."

"I've never seen such a wonderful baptism," I breathed. "My brother does baptisms, and they're so proper you could sleep through them. He doesn't immerse people in water, of course."

"Ah, yes, your brother, the minister. Perhaps you could help me some. I'm planning on bringing Owen here home. And cajoling your brother not to whip him for running off. Tell me, can he be cajoled?"

I thought of Richard, thin and tall and prim, with his tight mouth and his stern demeanor. Richard was the last person on earth who could be cajoled. He would have to forgive Owen, and he had never forgiven anybody in his life for anything. The only one who could make him smile was William.

"It depends, Nat, on how persuasive you can be," I said.

He smiled, showing gleaming white teeth. His eyes smiled, too, and I thought I could never fear him like I fear some of the negroes on our place. No, this man has goodness in him. "When are you coming?" I asked.

"Perhaps later on today," he suggested. "At dusk. I have found men to be most mellow at dusk."

Suppertime, I thought. Richard is most mellow at suppertime. A glass of port, a good cut of meat, yes. He'll be mellow at dinnertime. "I won't say anything," I told Nat. "I'll keep it secret. I do know that Mother Whitehead thinks much of you. She always wants to hire you on. You have a friend in our house."

We parted. Violet chatted all the way home, but I scarce heard her. I could not yet wrap my mind around the fact that I had met the one and only Nat Turner. And he was coming, this very day, to our house. And then I thought, Richard would not be rude. He would not dare. By tomorrow it would be all over the county that Nat Turner had come to our house and brought a runaway slave home and asked for mercy. One reverend to another. And no matter what people thought of Turner's power as a minister, well, they knew of Richard's. They respected Richard. And as their minister, he could do no less than be cordial to Turner, could he? Because Turner had come to him, beseeching him. And as a true man of the cloth, Richard could not turn him away.

It came to me then that it was just this that Nat Turner was counting on. That he had already figured it out in his head. And he was counting on the fact that Richard, a graduate of Hampden-Sydney College, would already know this.

Six

❦

We heard the knock on the back door halfway through the repast that served as Sunday supper. The house, which was rambling and three story, with rooms that went off in directions that looked as if no architect ever drew up the plans, was large and comfortable. A newcomer could get lost in it. But it had that necessity every Southern mansion had—a center hall, which kept the air coming through on even the hottest of days.

At first, when I heard the knocking I thought, *Oh good, Nat Turner knows enough to come to the back door. That will give him points with Richard.* And then I thought, *No, it's Owen's idea. He was in charge of an-*

swering the door and sending negroes to the back when he was here.

Violet came into the dining room, careful not to look at me. She'd been "doing the doors" since Owen ran away. "Master Richard, there's someone to see y'all."

"Who is it?" Richard growled. "You know I don't like to interrupt my meals for guests."

"It's Nat Turner, suh. That negro preacher."

"I'm not interested in talking with him. Can't even control the onlookers at his baptism. Tell him to come another time. Offer him some iced tea and tell him to go."

Before supper Richard had cross-examined Violet and me about the baptism and had been outright horrified at the behavior of those boys who had come to see it. "What kind of a minister is that?" he'd asked of no one in particular. But I couldn't help feeling that he was glad to hear our report. And that he'd used me as a spy.

"But, suh," Violet protested now, "he's got *Owen* with him."

"Who?"

"Owen, suh, who done run off. He's got him."

Mother's knife and fork clattered onto her plate. She

had missed Owen dearly. She started to get up. "Richard, if you don't go, I will. It's our Owen, for heaven's sake."

"I know," he growled, and pushed back his chair. "Sit, Mother, I'll handle it."

But she insisted on getting up. I got to my feet and helped her.

Violet spoke again. "He says, suh, that he wants to see Miz Catharine. And Miz Harriet, as well as you."

Richard tore the white dinner napkin from his shirt-front. "Oh, he does, does he? Does he know he isn't quite running things around here?"

Violet simply curtsied and went out of the room to the glass-enclosed, plant-filled solarium in back of the house. Mother Whitehead and I followed.

They stood there like two lost travelers. Nat Turner had dressed in clean trousers and a patched but fresh shirt and weskit. His shoes were polished. Owen's old clothes had been replenished. They turned as we came in. I thought I saw Owen cower a bit at the sight of my brother and make a move as if to get down on his knees, but Nat held him up firmly by the shoulders.

For a moment all was terrible silence. Then Mother Whitehead spoke and held out her arms in a welcoming embrace. "Owen, so you have come home to us. Welcome, child, I have missed you so!" That was her way. After all, she had trained him up since he was a knee baby.

He started toward her but did not get far. He had to get by Richard first, and Richard grabbed his arm in a fierce grip that bound him. "Home, are you?" he said in a voice of controlled anger.

"Yes, sir," Owen said quietly.

"And so what did you find in the outside world? Did you like it?"

"No, sir."

"How many meals of hominy and bacon did you have? How much pot likker? Did you sleep on a straw mattress or on the rough ground? Did you sleep at all? Answer me! No, don't speak. I suppose you went about stealing things from good folks' plantations. How many chickens did you steal? Well?" He gave Owen a little shake. "How many of our neighbors do I have to pay off for what you stole from them? You'll tell me, you will. And for every ten dollars you'll get ten stripes. You hear?"

Nat Turner spoke up then. "That's why I'm here, Mr. Whitehead," he said. "To tell you that he was with me the whole time. At my master's. He was fed and he worked and he stole nothing. You don't owe nobody anything.

Mr. Travis owes you for the work he did. It was as if you hired him out."

He reached inside his breeches pocket and drew out some silver coins and put them on a nearby glass-topped table. "That's for his hire, sir. Mr. Travis wants you to have it."

"Are you making a fool out of me?" Richard asked.

"No, sir," Nat Turner said.

I could watch his face, hear the even tone in his voice, and tell how he despised Richard. "Mr. Travis's only wish is that you don't whip Owen for running off. He says if you don't want him anymore, he'll buy him from you. He does a full day's work, he says."

The wind went out of Richard's sails. He released Owen. "What I do with my property is my business," he said. "If I want to whip him, I'll whip him. And it's none of Travis's business how I do with my negroes."

"You know better, Richard," Mother Whitehead said kindly. "Here in this county it is everybody's business how everybody else treats their negroes." And she stepped forward and put an arm around Owen's shoulder and patted his head. "Violet, go and take Owen into the kitchen and give him some good vittles. No, Harriet, you stay here, this is family business. I only wish Margaret were here instead of gallivanting around all the time."

And then to Nat Turner, "I am Mother Whitehead, Nat Turner. As you must have heard by now, I am near totally blind. But what the eyes can't see, the heart can. Anyway, my son, Richard, runs things around here and is the one to be reckoned with. But on this one matter I shall overstep him. Because I've known Owen since he was born. I am most pleased to meet you. I am the one always writing to Mr. Travis and asking him to hire *you* out to *me.* I have already asked him to allow me to buy you. But he refuses. It says much about your character and your work."

"Yes, ma'am," Nat answered.

"Richard has his reputation to keep. Both as a property and slave owner in Southampton County and a leading Methodist minister."

I heard Richard sigh heavily.

"I can tell you, Nat Turner, that it is not an easy path my son has taken. To head up a plantation with sixty slaves and be a minister who stands for forgiveness and love is a double duty most could not perform. I hope you will tell others how Richard manages it. Your young friend is safe and welcomed home. We thank you for what you have done for us. And I promise you that very soon you will be working, for hire, in this very house. May we offer you something cool to drink?"

Nat said no. He left then. Richard glared at Mother, who, thank heaven, could not see the look. But he could not go against her wishes. And he knew it.

Seven

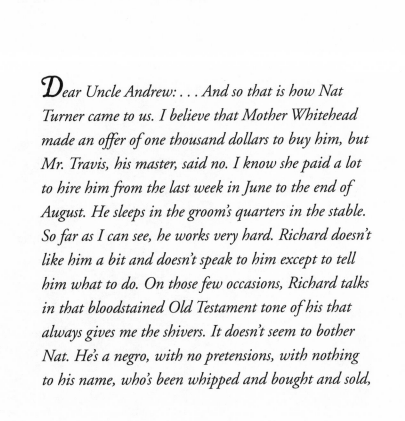

*D*ear Uncle Andrew: . . . And so that is how Nat Turner came to us. I believe that Mother Whitehead made an offer of one thousand dollars to buy him, but Mr. Travis, his master, said no. I know she paid a lot to hire him from the last week in June to the end of August. He sleeps in the groom's quarters in the stable. So far as I can see, he works very hard. Richard doesn't like him a bit and doesn't speak to him except to tell him what to do. On those few occasions, Richard talks in that bloodstained Old Testament tone of his that always gives me the shivers. It doesn't seem to bother Nat. He's a negro, with no pretensions, with nothing to his name, who's been whipped and bought and sold,

traded and abused, and his voice isn't bloodstained at
all. He makes you believe that God is forgiving and
good. I'd rather believe in his God than Richard's
God, who is always angry and ready to punish and
send us to hell forever. Please write soon.
    Your loving niece, Harriet

"Another letter to Andrew?" Mother Whitehead
asked.

"Yes, ma'am."

"I'm not so sure it's good, a young girl like you corresponding with a half-wit uncle like him. Why can't you
be more like Margaret and have friends in the neighbor-
hood? You see, she's spent the weekend at the Gerards'
again. She has a true friend in Emilie, her own age. I hear
she's bringing Emilie home for the week."

"Mother Whitehead, in the first place Uncle Andrew
isn't a half-wit. He's quite sane and he has many people
of eminence in England as his friends. Not only my father's old business contacts, but people who are artists
and writers and such. And as for Margaret, the only reason she's having Emilie for the week is because Emilie is
going out of her senses at home, because Richard put her

mother out of his church and her mother is carrying on so about it."

Mother Whitehead's blue eyes went wide. The head of half-white, half-chestnut curls shook in a negative way. "Put Charlotte out of the church? But why? The woman bakes the best upside-down cake I ever tasted. We need her for our bake sales."

"Upside-down cakes don't get you into heaven." Richard came out onto the veranda where we were talking.

"But she just lost her husband. Why did you put her out?" Mother Whitehead asked.

He leaned down and kissed her forehead. "You know I won't discuss the sins of other people in front of y'all. I'm on my way now to fetch Margaret and the girl. We ought to be home within the hour. We'll have dinner. Where is that darky today, Mother? What's he working on?"

"The table from the library that used to be your father's. You know how it's always falling down. The round, oak one. He used to put his favorite books on it."

"I'd throw it out," Richard said. "Get a new one. We can afford it, Mother."

"It was your father's," she said again. And that was all she said, except "Nat Turner is in the library working on it."

Richard left. I had a pretty good idea what Charlotte Gerard had done that was so terrible that Richard had put her out of his church. I knew that her husband had just died and she was surrounded by a lot of gossip. About two months ago, Cecil R. Gerard, her husband, had fallen from his horse and hurt his back. Charlotte had sent for Dr. Gordon to come and fix him up. He was on the way to recovery when pneumonia set in. The good doctor had stayed in the overseer's cottage on the plantation. Two weeks ago, Cecil R. Gerard had died. In his will he left the plantation to Charlotte, on one condition.

As long as she did not marry again, the plantation was hers. If she did, it went to Emilie, the daughter, and Charlotte was not to enjoy its benefits in any way. Which meant, the lawyers said, that she was not to live in the big house at all.

What happened was that Charlotte moved into the overseer's house with Dr. Gordon. She did not marry, so the plantation was still hers. She ran it by day and slept with Dr. Gordon by night and that, I assumed, was why Richard had evicted her from his congregation.

Emilie was mortified. And crying all the time. And to give my sister, Margaret, some credit, she had remained a true friend to her but did not know what to do. And so now she was bringing Emilie home to us. As if we knew how to help her, with all our peculiarities and underlying hatreds.

I waited until Richard climbed into the gilt and cherrywood brougham, which was pulled by two thoroughbred horses and driven by Chancy the groom, to excuse myself from Mother Whitehead. And then I went to the library to seek out Nat Turner. He'd been with us only a week, but in that time I'd discovered that he had answers to questions I didn't even know I had.

⌒✎⌒

I sat down in a chair in the corner and just watched him for a while. He hummed while he worked. A low, deep-throated hymn. And with the windows open and the chirping of the birds outside and the buzzing of a bumble-bee nearby it sounded peaceful. This house was seldom peaceful.

"Is that a church song?" I asked.

"It's an old spiritual," he said. "If you don't have a church, it's still all right to sing it."

"Do you have a church?"

"No, little missy. I preach wherever the good Lord allows me to preach. I hold my Bible classes under the big tree behind the fruit and vegetable stands in Jerusalem."

I nodded. "You believe in a different God than my brother Richard believes in," I told him.

"How's that?"

"All Richard talks about is how God is going to punish us. Your God loves us. I never once heard Richard talk about a God who loves and forgives us. How am I supposed to know which God to believe in?"

He smiled. "Some of us take our whole lives pondering that question out," he answered. "Why don't you just go ahead and treat God as you'd want Him to be and see how He responds?"

"What makes you think He'd respond to me?"

"Why wouldn't He?"

"I'm just a no-count little girl on a plantation in the South. There are probably thousands of others like me."

He went on working. "Did you ever see snow?"

"Of course."

"Did you know that out of millions and millions of flakes, no two are fashioned alike?"

I just stared at him as if he'd taken leave of his senses.

"If God can do that with snowflakes, then don't you think He can do that with thousands of little girls on plantations in the South? Make them different and individual?"

I was staring at him.

"And if God makes all those little girls individual, don't you think He'd bother to respond to them as such?"

"Yes," I said.

He shrugged. "He responds to me," he said, "and I'm just one more black man amongst millions in this country. He responds because I talk to Him. Not as a punisher, but as a friend."

I was becoming frightened now and so I gave the conversation a new turn.

"Emilie is coming to stay the week. Emilie Gerard. Do you know who she is?"

More smiles. "I know," he said in a singsongy way.

"Do you think Richard should have put her mother out of his church?"

"It's his church. Though I always thought church was the place for sinners. And that we were all sinners. Even Richard." He started humming again.

ANN RINALDI

Now I started to feel better. "Thank you," I said. "Things are starting to look more clear to me already. I mean, I was brought up to think of God as Richard, only bigger. I'm starting to figure that He isn't."

He never stopped working. "There is some little thing you can do for me," he said quietly. "Your father's old gun room is next door. I had to go in there the other day to see how the twin table like this was put together. On the other table was a map of Southampton County. Do you suppose you could, secretly, within the next few weeks, bring it here for me to borrow? I don't want to take it out of the house. I just want to study it a while."

"Of course," I said as I got up.

"And tell no one."

"Yes, I'll do that. Are you taking a trip?"

"You could say that. I need to be more familiar with the roads and the woods."

I walked to the door and stopped. "If you see Emilie Gerard around during the next week, talk to her, will you?" I begged. "She is the most confused human being lately."

"I sure will, missy, I sure will."

Eight

Nat Turner ate breakfast in the kitchen with the household help. With Connie and Owen and Violet and Winefred, who was the cook, and Ormond. They all liked him. He was polite and pleasant. Winefred heaped his plate with food twice, and he had all the hot coffee he could drink.

He was a likely negro, the kind you wanted to do things for. Today I would get the map of the county for him from Father's gun room.

At our table in the dining room, I stared at Emilie. It was Thursday, but she wore a Sunday frock with a pink sash around the middle. Her hair was pulled back from her brow and tied with a bow. She was fifteen, the same age as Margaret, yet this morning there was a weariness about her that made her appear ancient.

"Have some fruit, dear," Mother Whitehead said.

"I'm really not hungry," she answered.

"Richard," Mother appealed to him, "she must eat."

"I'm not her brother, Mother," he reminded her. "And I'm not her minister anymore since she refuses to come to my church. So I can't even see to the starvation of her soul."

Emilie came to life then. "I would come, if you hadn't thrown my mama out. How can I come now, without her?"

"You should come *for* her," he said evenly. "You should come to pray for her. Haven't my past sermons taught you anything?"

"Yes," Emilie threw at him, "that you pray for those who are close to God, and those who aren't, who *need* Him, you toss away like garbage."

Everyone went silent. Hooray, I said to myself. How I wish I had the courage to talk to Richard like that. As for my brother, he looked as if someone had thrown a pitcher of cold water in his face. But he kept his dignity. He even smiled.

"If you were one of my sisters, I'd have the pleasure

of sending you to kneel on the stones out back and then spend the day in your room," he said mildly. "But you're not, so I suppose I must take the insult. Unless, of course, you are prepared to apologize."

Emilie wasn't. "I think I'll have some fruit now," she said. "I find I have an appetite after all."

"Come, come, children, don't fight," Mother White-head cajoled. But she said it in a pleasant way so that, if you knew her, you knew that she was enjoying the whole thing. "Emilie, that isn't what you came here for, is it? To quarrel with the reverend?"

"No, ma'am," Emilie said quietly. "I came to visit y'all. And to ask him a favor."

"Well then, after we're finished, why don't you all go into the library and talk, you and Richard? You'll find him a true man of the cloth, I promise you. Right, Richard?"

He had to agree. He was more fearful of his mother than he was of God. So when breakfast was over he kissed Mother Whitehead on the forehead and he and Emilie went into the library, and he closed the door. Only later did I find out, through Margaret, what she wanted from him.

She wanted him to come to their plantation and speak to her mother. To turn her around so that she would end her affair with Dr. Gordon. Richard told her he had done that already, in church. Emilie said, "Do it again, in the parlor of our plantation. Please."

Richard said no. "Once is enough," he said. "I'll not kneel at your mother's feet. She'll have no respect for me. She knows right from wrong." And he said no, too, when Emilie asked him for a second chance for her mother; to let her return to church. When he said no to that, Emilie said that she wouldn't return then, either.

Richard told her that everyone has their own God to answer to. And He was a very vengeful God when treated like such. And her mother, and perhaps she, too, would burn in hell for taking such a stand.

Emilie cut short her visit. Margaret and I were both in the room when she packed her things that very afternoon. "I don't know how you stand it in a house with him," she told us. "I don't know," she said, looking at me, "how you stand having a brother be a minister in the first place."

I told her it wasn't easy, that it was awkward at best. That people expected you to walk around with your eyes downcast, praying all the time.

"And they're always asking, 'What would your brother say?'" I told her.

Margaret said I was daft. "You get respect," she told Emilie. "I find that people respect me more because my brother is a man of the cloth."

"I earn my own respect," I told Emilie. "I don't ride the coattails of someone else."

Margaret looked as if she wanted to slap me. "It helps in school," she said through clenched teeth. "The teachers are always trying to please me because of Richard. Most of them are in his congregation."

"So *that's* how you get your good marks," I said in astonishment. "And Mother Whitehead and Richard think it's because you've earned them."

"Do you two always fight like this?" Emilie asked.

"Yes," I said. "You could say there's no love lost between us."

"I wish I had a sister," she said wistfully, "just to commiserate with. Just to confide in. I'd never fight with her."

And then Margaret said the one thing I knew was always on her mind. "She's my half sister," she said.

That brought silence into the room. Emilie finished her packing.

"What will you do when you go home?" I asked her. "Live in the house alone with all the servants?"

"I don't know," she answered. "I haven't come to that

bridge yet. Mayhap I'll move in with my aunt Marie Claire in Jerusalem. I'll let you all know."

Mother had Nat Turner drive Emilie home. Margaret went with them. Before they left I sneaked some words with Nat Turner. "Talk to her," I begged. "Tell her that God is not vengeful. Tell her that He is a forgiving God, please."

He promised he would.

Nine

I didn't give the map of Southampton County to Nat Turner for another two weeks. Though he was an acknowledged minister, I knew it was wrong to do so.

The reasons why I'd learned with my ABCs. One did not give maps or plans or letters or any reading material to nigras. It was all part of the Southern belief system that they did not know how to read, of course, though quite a few of them did. Those who did were considered dangerous and to be watched. It was that simple.

They were to be suspected of any motive. Did Turner want the map so he could rob houses? I could not forgive myself, at first, for thinking that.

But I had another problem.

Suppose the family saw me walking around with the map in my hands? What reason would I give as to why I had it? I was not known to be studious. Pleasant had all she could do to be patient with me.

And then my reason for borrowing the map came to me. I would go to Pleasant first and tell her that it was time for me to understand Southampton County. Wasn't it? She would be surprised but happy. And say yes to my "borrowing" the map to study over the remaining weeks of summer.

"Why I'll know all the roads and small towns' names and who lives where, and creeks and streams and sign-posts," I told her. "And then do you know what, Pleasant? We'll go on a ride, just you and I, when the fall comes. A picnic, and I'll see all the places I studied about."

She laughed, and tossed her chestnut curls. "We'll have to be escorted. You know Richard won't let us wander around alone."

I shrugged. "Owen can be our escort. He's big and strong now."

It was agreed. And as if the Lord had blessed my plans, the post came early the next morning. And there was a letter from Uncle Andrew that I quickly snatched out of the mass of mail that was put on the table in the hallway.

I had written to him about how I was going to lend Nat Turner the map of Southampton County. Quickly I scanned the letter.

My dear, I can't give you a viable opinion of slavery or of dealing with the slaves in general or in particular. But from my vague memories I can tell you that a slave who knows how to read and write is never innocent of planning or conniving, no matter how likable he seems. I would watch myself with Nat Turner. In many ways it sounds as if he is trying to get information from you. For what, I don't know. But I'd venture that he is planning something. That is only my opinion, of course, and I am only a sixty-eight-year-old man for whom the very idea of slavery seems dim and quaint. And oh yes. Don't ever let him have the key to the gun room.

It was the first time Uncle Andrew disagreed with me on anything. And it was not very forceful, so that

ANN RINALDI

morning, after reading the letter, I went immediately to
the gun room. It was locked, of course. But I knew
where the key was. Everybody did, apparently even Nat
Turner, who had entered the gun room to look at the
twin table, so I wondered at the necessity of locking it.
I pulled over a chair in the hallway, stepped up on it,
and retrieved said key from the top of the doorjamb and
opened the door.

I had always wondered why Father kept such an array
of guns. There were at least twenty muskets and rifles,
twelve flintlock pistols, six fowling pieces, six swords, two
cutlasses, and plenty of powder and lead. My father must
have been a prime marksman, too, because there were at
least eight trophies for shooting. It all impressed me
much but not in a pleasant way.

Then I focused my attention on the map on the
round oaken table in the corner. There it was, spread out.
I studied it for a minute. In all the years I'd lived here I
had never really looked at the map of Southampton
County.

For a moment I had my doubts again. But then I
folded the map carefully and put it in my apron pocket.
I would ask Nat Turner, once more, why he needed it.

And then, on my way out of the room, another

phrase rang in my head like a church bell on Sunday. *Don't ever let him have the key to the gun room.*

How did Uncle Andrew know the gun room was locked? Oh, the question begged an answer. But there was none. He'd never been to this house! He'd never even been to America!

Silly, I told myself, *all gun rooms are locked. Who leaves one open?*

Who? Just who?

I waited until after breakfast, until after everyone had settled down and gone to their appointed tasks. I wrote some letters for Mother Whitehead, then settled her on the veranda where she would stay until it became too hot. I fetched her knitting. She could still knit, though near blind. She just needed help picking out the colors. And she now excused me for an hour or so. All the while I had the map of Southampton County, folded neatly, in my apron pocket.

I found Nat Turner working on a chair in the library.

"Good morning, missy."

"Good morning." Margaret was looking at books at the other end of the room. She wore her blue silk robe over her pajamas. What must Nat Turner think? I should talk to her later, I told myself. I should ask Mother Whitehead to talk to her. No, I should have Richard say something. Would they tell me to mind my own business? It *was* my business, wasn't it? Why did I know it was wrong and not Margaret?

The answer was that Margaret knew.

What was it Uncle Andrew had said? *I can tell you that a slave who knows how to read and write is never innocent of planning or conniving.*

She stood up now, Margaret did. "I found it," she said of the book in her hand. "*Tristan.* I knew it was here." Triumphantly she marched from the room. Nat did not look at her. He kept his eyes lowered, and I knew this was bad, this was worse than if he had looked at her. This showed that he did not trust himself to look at her.

"I have your map," I told him. And I drew it from my pocket.

He took it and spread it on the floor. He was most pleased and thanked me. He studied it for a moment and a brown finger traced over the roads while his lips moved silently.

"How long can I keep it for?" he asked.

I hadn't thought about that. I thought he only wanted to look at it, perhaps for ten minutes, and when I told him this he shook his head.

"I need it for at least three weeks," he told me.

I became irritated, then. Three weeks! And what was I supposed to do if someone asked why it was gone? Pleasant knew I had it now. And Nat wouldn't even do me the honor of telling me why he needed it so badly.

"I can't let you have it that long," I told him. "It's been right there, out in the open on the table forever. If my brother, Richard, goes in there for anything, he'll notice that it isn't there anymore and ask why. Not that he *needs* it. But it's really the only one within ten miles and people sometimes come and ask him to use it. People who are planning fishing or hunting trips. And besides, it's special because it belonged to my father."

He nodded slowly but never took his eyes from the map.

"Are you planning a fishing trip?" I asked. I didn't say *hunting* because negroes weren't allowed to have guns.

"You could say that, after a fashion."

I met his eyes with mine. And mine were full of hurt because he was holding back with me.

He gave a small smile. "I am a fisher of men, like the Lord told Saint Peter he would be doing from here on in. I am going to stop at plantations and preach of the God that loves us."

I let out a sigh. Of course.

"Well, if that's what you're going to do, then I have an idea," I told him. "My sister-in-law, Pleasant, Richard's wife, thinks I have this map to study for schoolwork. But since it is so valuable I think that it should be copied, and the original should be put back on the table in the library."

He nodded, not quite understanding.

"I know that Pleasant has some very thin tracing paper. I can get it from her and then all I have to do is put it over the top of the map and trace it onto the thin paper."

His eyes went wide, understanding. "You would do that? For me?"

"Yes. But you'd still have to give the traced copy back to me, because I'm supposed to be studying it for school."

"Yes." He looked at me, a piercing look, one that took in more than I was willing to give him.

And so we came to our agreement, which was at the cornerstone of the events that followed. *No, Uncle, I never gave him the key to the gun room. I gave him something worse.*

Ten

"I think it's a wonderful idea," Pleasant said to me as she rustled around amongst her embroidery things to find the tracing paper. She was a much-talented woman, my sister-in-law. She once told me that she had a rich inner life, which had nothing to do with religion. "It keeps me sane," she confessed.

Ah, there was the tracing paper. She gave me two pieces. "Richard will like that you don't want to dirty or otherwise wrinkle the original map," she said as I left her room.

It took me two days to trace Southampton County because Mother Whitehead came up with a parcel of letters that had to be written, of a sudden. My hands were ink-stained before I finished, and I was tired of holding a pen.

She owed people letters, she told me. And they were very important. One was to Jenkins, Middleton, and Pierce, her cotton factors who sold her cotton and took 4 percent for doing so:

Dear Sirs: This is to ascertain that I will be signing on with you for another year, as pleased as I have been with your reputation for caution and reserve. I was pleased with the price of forty-five cents a pound brought by my fine crop of cotton and even the coarse grade that brought thirty-one cents a pound. Let's hope prices rise again this year and that English brokerage houses don't collapse, that there are no reports of bad weather, and no king of importance abdicates. I will write again soon to order my list of wheat, flour, salt, coffee, tools, and all other manner of items the plantation does not produce. . . .

And so it was more than two days before I gave my rendition of the map to Nat Turner. I told no one, except, of course, Violet. Her eyes went wide at the telling. "What," she asked, "did he say he was going to do with it?"

"He said he was going to stop at plantations and preach to the people how the Lord loves us. And is a forgiving God," I told her. It had sounded so good, so right, when Nat said it. Now it sounded empty and flat.

Violet said nothing for a moment. Then, "I think we should pay a visit to my grandmother."

I drew in my breath. Her grandmother was Cloanna, the oldest woman on the place. She was grandmother to all the slave children. Nobody knew exactly how old Cloanna was, but she used to be the cook and everybody who remembered still talked about how wonderful the dishes were that she turned out. They said nobody could ever cook like Cloanna again.

Now, too old to work anymore, she spent her mornings on the wooden porch of her cabin, stitching clothes for the little slave children. And her afternoons, trimming the ends off beans or shucking corn. She would not let her hands be idle, lest the devil use them for his workshop, she had told us.

Not many people on the plantation visited her. Truth

to tell, she had "the gift." She knew things. And since everyone, even all the slaves, had secrets they didn't want brought out into the open, she kept those secrets for them. I like to think she stitched them into the clothing she made for the little folk.

She could always be counted on to keep a body's secrets. So people told her things.

Up until now I hadn't had any secrets. Oh, how I wished I had. When she discovered that about me, she just leaned back in her ancient rocking chair and laughed. "Go get yourself some secrets, girl. Life ain't interestin' if'n you doan have any."

Now I had one. And I was not as all-out thrilled as I thought I would be. I was more frightened than anything. The secret was a burden, not a joy. I decided I would say nothing to Cloanna. I would see if she could discover it on her own. And I warned Violet not to say anything, either.

But Violet was troubled by what I had done. I could tell. And whenever Violet was troubled, it was enough for her just to go and visit Cloanna, even if she never said a word.

Sure enough, there was Cloanna in her rocking chair, snipping the ends off beans. Her face was a map I'd like to trace. I'd love to see where it would take me. And I'd love to see where she had been.

"What you two doin' here in the slave quarters on such a beautiful day?" she scolded. "Why ain't you rompin' in the meadow, or pickin' some flowers, or fishin' in the pond?"

"I'm too old to romp," Violet told her.

"Humph. When I wuz your age I hooked my skirts up and went wadin' in the pond."

"I've done that when I picked cattails," Violet said. "Massa Richard said if he caught me at it again he'd whip my legs."

"He did, did he? He's gotten terrible persnickety since he become a preacher. When he wuz a whippersnapper boy I used to box his ears when he come inta my kitchen and stole my fresh-baked bread and just-churned butter. Ask him about that sometime if'n you want to see his face go red."

"No thank you, Grandma, I don't talk like that to Massa Richard."

"Well he needs somebody to talk to him like that. You there, little Miz Harriet, the cat got your tongue this day? Why you so quiet?"

"No reason," I told her.

"No reason to lie to Cloanna, missy. She knows the difference. It's heavy, ain't it?"

"What?"

"That secret you're totin' round inside you. It's bearin' down on you. You finally got yourself a first-rate secret an' it ain't so much fun now, is it?"

Tears came to my eyes. "No," I admitted.

"Listen to me, chile." And she leaned forward. "I doan know all. But somethin' tells me it's about paper. An' lines on the paper. 'Portant lines. An' you stole that paper. Is old Cloanna right?"

"I didn't really steal it," I said.

"Now you lyin' to Cloanna. It's bad to lie to people, chile, but it'll get you right inta hell to lie to me. Didn't anybody ever tell you that?"

"No," I said.

She went back to snipping the ends off her beans. "Would you do as I say if'n I say to destroy that paper you stole?"

I looked at her blankly.

"Doan give me that dumblike look. If'n there's anythin' you ain't, it's dumb. Well, would you do as I say if I told you to destroy it?"

"I don't know," I answered.

"Well I'm sayin' it, anyways. Destroy it. No good will come out of you stealin' it when it ain't yours to have. Look, little Harriet chile, I feel it in my ninety-two-year-old bones. Like when the sky gathers black around me and it threatens rain. My knees hurt. My back hurts. My wrists hurt. Somethin' bad gonna happen round heah, and I want no part of it. So you better watch your p's an' q's and doan go foolin' 'round any. Now I've said my piece. Go, go and leave me alone."

"Why can't you tell us more?" I pushed.

"'Cause I the keeper of secrets round heah, tha's why," she answered firmly. "Now go, the both of you. An' leave me with my beans."

We left, sadly. "I'd like to know what secrets she carries about people around here," I told Violet.

"I'll wager she carries them to the grave," she said.

"What do you suppose she meant about something bad going to happen around here?"

"She just wants to scare the boots off us," Violet said.

But we were quiet walking home. And I think we both knew not to distrust Cloanna. Too many times when she predicted something, it had come true. Like the time she told Richard to get all the cows in the barn one midsummer night, that the wolves were going to attack. Richard only scoffed at her. And the next morning he had three dead calves lying in the pasture.

Richard never discounted anything she said again.

Eleven

Of a sudden, I felt myself getting a fever. I was hot and yet my hands and feet were freezing. I left Violet to her chores as soon as we got back from slaves' row, and I headed straight to the groom's quarters in the stable, where Nat was living, to give him the map. I never paid much mind to what Cloanna said. She said it mostly for the negro children, anyway.

The map was burning a hole in my apron pocket. I was tired of the thought of it by now, and I wanted to be shed of it.

It was about three o'clock in the afternoon, I reckon, but there was no one about the barnyard. The sun poured down on the dust, raising it up into choking air.

I longed to take my clothes off and go for a dip in the pond. I looked around. There was a parcel of slaves in the cotton field in back of the slave quarters. And another tending to the apple trees in the orchard. But they weren't singing as they usually did when they worked. It was just too hot and there was nothing to sing about.

Nat Turner was not in his quarters. I stood and looked around. It was very neat. It had a fireplace, a desk, an oil lamp, and straw ticking.

On the desk was a pad of paper and on it was a list of names. I glanced at it. *Mrs. Whitehead, Richard, Pleasant, baby William, Margaret and Harriet, Violet, and all the house negroes but Owen, take him with us, he's angry enough. Make it quick and go on to the Jacobs place, two miles north.*

I felt my heart beating. Make it quick? What were we all doing listed on that paper? Was he going to gather us together and preach to us?

"What are you doing here, missy?"

His voice. I turned, my hands trembling, and I faced him. "I brought you the map," I said. "I couldn't find you. No one is about. So I thought I'd bring it here."

His eyes went from the paper with the names on the

desk to me. I pulled the map out of my apron pocket and handed it to him. He unfolded it carefully. It was very quiet, and I could hear Mother Whitehead's windmill *clack, clack, clack*ing in the fields, a sound I usually took for granted. I heard a cow moo, a dog bark. Suddenly sounds I took for granted all stood out against the starkness of the day for me, each demanding to be heard, as if for the first, or last, time.

He glanced, briefly, at the map. "You went to see Cloanna," he said. It was a statement, not a question.

"Yes."

"You talked to her about this."

"No. I never mentioned it. You don't have to with Cloanna. She just knows things."

He scowled, and it was as if God was scowling at me. "What do you mean, she *knows* things?"

"She has the gift. She can sense what troubles you have. And she can—"

"You had troubles? Giving me the map?"

"I never told her that. I never even told myself that. But yes, I was confused about it."

"Why? I told you I was going to visit these houses and preach to these people, didn't I? White people need to be preached to. They don't know God. They go to church all fancified in their tall hats and bonnets and eye each other up and gossip about who did what all week and simper at each other and think that God is going to listen to them. That's not what God wants! Do you know what God wants from them?"

I was beginning to get frightened. "No."

"He wants them to come to their senses. He wants them to let their negroes free. That's what He wants."

I drew in my breath.

"And that's what I aim to tell them."

I nodded my head in agreement.

"So what did she say about the map, then, to get you in such a state of mind?"

"She didn't know it was a map. She only knew it was a paper—" I saw him staring at me and stopped.

He nodded his head, folded the map, put it in the pocket of his shirt, and then stepped over to the desk and added Cloanna's name to the list on the paper.

"She's one of the Goody Two-shoes around here, much as she tries to be different. You see what a nice cabin she has? What good food and how she is regularly supplied? You think that comes from being a trouble-maker? A dissident? No, those who make trouble and shake things up are lucky to get bread and water. *But to us it's a feast for angels!* Do you understand?"

"I think so," I answered.

"Cloanna will be preached to," he said. "When I am finished with her, she will understand."

Twelve

Before Nat Turner could put his plan into motion, however, another incident happened that gave us all pause about our practice of slavery.

Two slaves ran off from the Gerard plantation down the road, the one where Mr. Gerard had died and his wife, Charlotte, was now living with his doctor in a cottage on the grounds. The place from whence Emilie came.

"It must be chaos there," Richard said at supper the evening I gave Nat the map. "I understand their overseer rules with an iron fist, which is why the slaves continually run away."

We had supper in near silence. Pleasant said she

thought Richard should take a ride over there and see what was going on. "Just your presence helps," she reminded him. "All you have to do is ride into a barnyard and it has a calming effect. The slaves all know who you are."

Richard puffed up at the compliment, as he was meant to do. "We'll see," he said.

Then a courier came with a note for Richard, brought to the table by Owen. Richard excused himself to sit there and read it, then raised his eyes and looked at his mother. "It's an invitation to all our slaves to witness a beating," he said.

Mother Whitehead scowled. "A beating?" she asked.

"Yes," Richard answered, as quietly as if it were an invitation to a barbecue. "A hundred lashes. Charlotte's overseer wants me to bring all our slaves to witness the whipping of Ebban, one of the slaves who ran away. It seems that he attacked one of the patrollers. They want to set an example."

"*Richard!*" exclaimed Pleasant. "You can't. You can't bring all the slaves."

"And why not?" he wanted to know.

"Because," she said. And oh I did admire the way she stood up to him. "Not the women, anyway. I mean, think of what that means. It means Violet and Cloanna and . . ." She was counting on her fingers.

Richard said, "I should think it a good thing for them to see."

"What about Nat Turner?" she asked.

"He doesn't belong to me," he said quickly. I think he was a little afraid of Nat Turner. "The overseer of Charlotte's says he wants to do this tomorrow. Get it over with. Charlotte," and he glanced again at the note, "adds a line here that says can we please fetch Emilie to stay over tonight as she doesn't want the girl to see this. I'll go fetch her. It isn't far." He stood up. "I'll go tell the courier yes to all of it."

"Da, Da," said baby William, waving his fat little arms. He was daft over his father. Pleasant set him down on the floor, and he toddled out of the dining room after Richard.

Richard brought Emilie home that night. "Mother won't put a stop to this," she said between tears when we had her safely ensconced upstairs. "She's so taken with Dr. Gordon, she cares about little else. She lets Harry, our overseer, handle everything, and he is such a cruel man.

When my father was alive, he kept him reined in, but now Harry is determined to have his way and make a show of it. Oh, I hate him, and Dr. Gordon, and everyone." She burst into tears and hid her face in the bedcover. She slept overnight with Margaret.

◦◦◦◦

The next morning at breakfast Emilie was composed at least, if not happy. Pleasant allowed her to play with baby William and even feed him breakfast, and it turned out she loved babies. It was William who got her to laughing again and who claimed her attention even while the big commotion of Richard's gathering the slaves was going on outside. And then, against a canopy of a great deal of dust and a symphony of low moaning, the slaves were herded out onto the road and driven like cattle, by Richard and other slaves whom he trusted, in the direction of the Gerards'.

Then our place was eerily silent, for the women had gone, too. Even Violet, who was half slave and half white. I personally knew she would not be able to take this.

I brought second rounds of breakfast coffee out to the veranda for Mother Whitehead and Pleasant, Emilie,

Margaret, and myself. There was also breakfast cake and I told Mother Whitehead how I thought Violet would never make it through without fainting.

"No man will live through one hundred lashes," Mother Whitehead said quietly, stirring sugar into her cup. "He'll die before they reach seventy-five. It's a calculated way to kill him."

"Violet is only half colored," I said. "The half of her that's white will cry and faint."

"The half of her that's white is likely stronger than the half that's colored," Mother Whitehead said. And it made me think that she knew who Violet's father was.

"What will they do if he dies?" Pleasant asked.

"Say it was accidental," Mother Whitehead answered calmly. "You are not allowed to murder your slave in this state, but if it is accidental, they can't blame you. Then likely they will burn him so no one can exhume the body and see how mauled he was with the whip."

She spoke so calmly, I wondered how many times she had seen this happen. We drank our coffee and continued to just sit there as if we were afraid to go back into the house when the servants weren't about. As if they owned it and we were just guests.

So we sat there. Pleasant rocked William and put him down for a morning nap in a cradle kept on the veranda for the purpose. Margaret fell asleep on the settee. Mother dictated a letter and I wrote it down. Emilie just sat there staring into space. Soon a strange smell started to fill the air.

Emilie sniffed and sat forward and looked around. "What is that?" she asked. "That vile smell?"

Mother Whitehead sniffed, too, with her delicate nose but kept silent.

I breathed in. It smelled like something rotten. "Like something dying," I said to Mother Whitehead.

Her blue eyes sought mine. And in an instant we both knew. And Emilie didn't. At first it seemed that Mother Whitehead was not going to tell her, but then she had a change of heart.

"They're burning him," she said.

At precisely that moment Nat Turner came from the cool inner house, like one of its shadows, stepping out onto the veranda. He just stood there, tall and quiet and knowing, looking at us. "Mayhap y'all best get inside," he suggested, "so you all don't get sick from that smell."

"A good idea, Nat," Mother Whitehead said. And for all their concern they could have been talking about the slaughter of pigs on the first cold day of winter.

He helped her up. He took her coffee cup and set it on the tray and handed the tray to me, and then took her arm and brought her inside. He brought her into the front parlor and closed whatever windows were open and even drew the curtains. Then he went outside to wake Margaret and fetch her, Emilie, and Pleasant inside. He carried in the cradle with William in it.

He took Margaret aside for a moment and spoke to her, low and soft, before he brought her in. I think he was explaining to her what the smell was. I think the calmness and reasoning in his voice prevented her hysterics. When he brought her in and sat her down, he offered to make a new pot of coffee, assuring Mother Whitehead that he knew how. She said yes, and oh how nice, and before we knew what had transpired, Nat brought the coffee in along with washed cups and more cake.

I tried to catch his glance, to see the expression on his face, but I could not. He was like a stone idol, carved out of granite by someone who had more memories than they could bear and was carving them on his face to get rid of them.

He left us there in the parlor with nothing to talk about now, with nothing to do but wait for something terrible to happen, only we didn't know yet what it was to be.

Thirteen

*D*ear Uncle Andrew: The half of Violet that is white was strong on the outside, pleasing Mother Whitehead, who thought she was strong through and through. Violet served us at supper that evening after she came home and her face was placid, as usual, and she had about her the wits that always carried her through, though she would scarce look at me, for fear her true feelings would show and she would make a disgrace of herself.

That night, after she went to her attic room, I heard her crying from my bedroom down the stairs. I waited a bit to be sure the house was settled, and then I went up to her.

"Oh, Harriet," she said, her face buried in the pillow, lest anyone should hear, "it was terrible. I would die before I would let your brother make me attend one of those happenings again. And do you know, speaking of Richard, what he did?"

I was afraid to ask, so she told me, anyway.

She told me that just before they burned the slave, Richard got up there and gave a sermon! He told of the command God had given the servants, concerning their masters. He said they should love and obey their masters. He quoted all those passages from the Bible about slaves and masters.

Oh, Uncle Andrew, Violet was terrified. "I'm half negro," she said. "Do all those things apply to me? Are you my mistress? Would you have me burned? Would you try to stop it if Richard wanted it? And how can anyone who considers himself an upright human being order or attend the burning of another human being?"

I didn't know what to say, Uncle Andrew. I never think of her as being colored, or my servant. She is just my friend, and more of a sister to me than Margaret. I don't understand this slavery business at all. But I do understand that Violet never should have been made *to go to this killing. After all, she is only three years older than I.*

Anyway, she didn't want me to leave her that night, so I got under the quilt with her and held her, and she was shaking. I have never before seen this girl frightened of anything. We both soon fell asleep and, since she gets up at five thirty in the morning, I was able to slip downstairs to my own bed in the early hours so Mother Whitehead didn't catch me with her.

Violet was up extra early that morning. And do you know what for? To burn the clothes she attended the burning in! She said they had that terrible smell on them and she could never wear them again. And sure enough they did smell. And so did the clothing of the other household help.

And when they saw what she was about, soon, one by one, they all came out with the clothing they had attended the burning in. And soon there was a great pile of clothing burning out in the barnyard pit. When Richard came down for breakfast he asked what was going on. And he became very angry when Violet told him.

"So you've all thrown out a good set of clothes, have you?" he asked the house slaves. None of them

answered. "Well, then you can just do without a set
of clothing for the rest of the summer and fall," he
directed.

They moaned and he went straight into the dining
room for breakfast. And later, Mother Whitehead
went into the kitchen to "address" the women who had
burned their clothing. She would send to town for new
fabric, she said, and each one of them could stitch up
their own clothes. But she did not want them to think
she was undermining her son, Richard. Richard was
not himself this morning and, if not for pride, would
take back the order. Did they understand?

They said yes. Massa Richard was the boss, but
they would still have new clothes. They understood.
And you know what, Uncle Andrew? I believe they
understood more than Mother Whitehead gave them
credit for.

The house was strangely quiet all that day. We
scarce looked at each other, as if we were ashamed to
acknowledge that we belonged to the white part of the
human race.

Emilie is staying with us for a while. Margaret
went back to school, so now I have only Emilie and
Violet to worry about. I spent the day trying to

*convince Violet that Emilie is not to blame for what
happened to the slave, even though it happened on her
mother's plantation.*

*Since Emilie doesn't want to go home yet, I am in
charge of her. She, too, seems not to want to let me out
of her sight. She even sat herself down next to me
when I wrote letters for Mother Whitehead. I know
Mother Whitehead wouldn't have wanted her there
since all her correspondence is private, so I sat Emilie
in a chair a bit away from us. I gave Emilie a book
of poetry and told her not to move or speak, because
then Mother Whitehead would know she was in
the room.*

*All went well. Except that Richard insisted, after
lunch, on reading from the Bible. He must have
known how upset we all were by yesterday's events,
because he assured us that the master is not to blame
for whipping his servant, but that* he is only doing
his duty as a Christian!

*By the time he was finished, both Violet and
Emilie were in tears. So I asked Connie in the kitchen
if we could make some taffy and she said yes. And we
spent the afternoon pulling taffy. Do you believe,
Uncle Andrew, that such a simple task helped us? It*

was more comforting than hearing those Bible passages of Richard's. Just as taking little William for a walk in his wagon helped. He fell asleep and it turned out that we were a help to Pleasant.

So we gave the afternoon some sanity after all and I wonder, Uncle Andrew, is life sane, as we tried to make it? Or is it insanity, as it was yesterday on the Gerard plantation? And why don't more people try to make it sane?

Or if it is full of sanity for them, why do they try to rip that sanity to pieces and impose their form of insanity? Can you help me understand?

You have lived a very long time, Uncle Andrew, and you must know some of these answers. Perhaps someday you can answer them for me. Because you have survived to be such a respected gentleman as you are, I wish you every good thing there is.

I wish you wonderful books to read and poetry inside your head and words there, too, that you may yet write and good afternoons filled with sunshine and laughter and a glass of wine that glimmers in the sun and peace and hope.

Your loving niece, Harriet

Fourteen

There is a grapevine of communication the negroes have that runs from plantation to plantation around here so that they know everything, sometimes before the white people know it.

The word started going around two days after the Gerard slave was burned to death. You could see it in the faces of the negroes, both outside the house and inside.

Usually there were good feelings between me and most of the negroes on the place. If not downright friendly, they always gave me a smile when we passed each other, or tipped a hat or nodded a head and acknowledged my presence.

This day, there was none of that. This day, they lowered their eyes or looked the other way.

I felt left out of the circle of their trust. I felt as if they were avoiding me. Violet, recovered now only so she could present a good face to do her chores and grateful to me for helping her recover, came over to me after breakfast when everyone was finding their place to hide themselves for the day.

Mother Whitehead retired to her space in the corner on the veranda where the clematis and the passionflower climbed and made a sweet-smelling curtain for her pleasure.

Pleasant went to her reading room to prepare lessons for me. Little William went for a walk with Owen. Margaret, who had come home out of fear and with Richard's blessing, and Emilie left to gather some flowers to make a bouquet. And Richard rode over to the Williams place, about five miles north of us, because Mrs. Williams was ailing and had asked for his prayers and comfort.

"Harriet, I must talk to you," Violet whispered.

"About what?"

"It's a secret. Don't speak so loud."

I lowered my voice. "Is it the same secret all the servants know about?"

"You know it, then?"

"No, but I know they have one. I can tell because they are all agitated. And because they won't look at me, as if looking at me will give it away."

She was pulling me toward the kitchen, where the morning dishes were being washed and dried, where preparations were already being made for lunch, potatoes being peeled, fruit arranged in a bowl, cake being mixed.

Usually when I walked through the kitchen, Winefred the cook would take a piece of whatever she was cooking and give it to me. And I would take it as if it were a sacrament and put it in my mouth. Because it was sort of a sacrament, a sign of friendship and love between black and white.

This day she was slicing leftover turkey. She turned her back to me.

Connie was scraping batter for cake into a pan. At this juncture she would always hand me the spoon and allow me to pause and lick the bowl.

This time she did not.

We did not hesitate, Violet and I. She pulled me through the kitchen and outside.

The sky was blue on this hot August morning and there was already a hint of September in the air. In the distance the pond glistened and ducks swam innocently. And slaves were gathering in the orchard to pick the beautiful apples that were bending down to them. I breathed deeply. I would spend this day outside. I would ride. Mayhap I'd take Emilie with me. Do her good.

"Did you hear me, Harriet?"

"No, I'm sorry, I was thinking I'd like to ride out today."

"Look, I think you heard, but you don't want to admit it, so I'll say it again. *There was a warning from Nat Turner to Owen, who passed it on. 'Look out and take care of yourselves. Something will happen before long.'*"

I snapped back into reality. "Nat Turner said that?"

"Yes. That's his message."

I felt dizzy. "Let me go. I must see him."

"What makes you think he wants to see a little white girl like you? After that burning the other day, I don't think he wants to see anybody."

"He wasn't angry the other day. He waited on us. Made us fresh coffee, brought us inside, away from the smell."

"He's part actor. And he knew he had to do it. And not display his anger. That if he displayed it at the wrong time, he would give himself away."

I did not understand. "Where is he?"

"Down at the orchard. Supervising the apple picking. He has strange men with him. Told Richard they are his friends and they'll help for the day. One of them is named Hark, another Will. I don't know if he'll talk to you."

"He'll talk to me." I broke away from her and ran to the orchard.

⟡

"Nat? Nat Turner?" I looked up into the apple tree and sure enough, there he was, near concealed by the branches. He was plucking apples and tossing them down to one of his men.

"Watch yourself, Hark, you almost missed that one," he said. "Can't have bruised apples. Bruised slaves, now, that's something different. But not bruised apples."

I waited until he came down from the tree, wiping his hands on a towel. "You want to talk with me, little Harriet? Come on over here by the fence. These lieutenants of mine have big ears."

They said things to scoff at him. He waved them off.

At the fence he offered me an apple, which I took, and then, with perfect white teeth, he bit into his own.

"Is there trouble over the map?" he asked.

"No. But Violet told me this morning about your message."

"Ah, yes. Did you receive it, then?"

"Was it for me, too?"

"Now what do you think? Haven't we been friends?"

"But what does it mean? 'Something will happen before long.' And 'Look out and take care of yourselves.'"

"It means just what it says. I do not talk in riddles. What did I tell you I was going to do?"

"Go to all the plantations and make the people listen while you preach."

"Exactly."

"Then why the 'Look out and take care of yourselves'?"

"Some people don't like to be preached at."

He was lying. I was sure of it. As sure as I knew that the apple I held in my hands was fresh and just off the tree. But if he was lying, what was the truth? What was he going to do that would make people have to look out for themselves?

"Do you still have the map?" I asked stupidly.

"Of course. You gave it to me. I shall keep it, always."

"But I told you I would need it back for my studies."
He said nothing.

The map. The map was the key to the whole thing he had planned, I decided. *And I had given him the map!* Suddenly I felt sick, nauseous. My eyes blurred. The apple trees danced in front of them. I had to get away from this man before he could tell that I was frightened of him. "I must go back to the house," I said. "I must help Mother Whitehead write some letters."

Fifteen

That night, that warm August night, when the night bugs screamed and the frogs in the pond croaked out their love songs and summer thunder rumbled on the horizon, I learned that Nat Turner and six of his men were going to eat barbecue and drink apple brandy on Cabin Pond.

I could have considered this an innocent pastime, except that that very night I learned from Owen all about Hark, Nat's "lieutenant," and his past.

It seems that Hark had been bought from the plantation where he grew up by Mr. Travis. The owner who sold him, sold away at the same time his mother and two sisters from whom he had never been separated a day in his life, and sent them to a plantation in Mississippi.

For a slave, Mississippi was the equivalent of hell. Slaves didn't live long in Mississippi.

Then, in the last eight years, Travis had sold off both Hark's wife and his son. Again to Mississippi.

This kind of story does not make for a good slave. This kind of story makes for the worst kind of anger in a slave. And Hark, being so close to Nat Turner now and planning on "making something happen," was enough to tell me that it was not going to be a good happening. Not at all.

I lay in my bed, the windows of my room open to admit the August air. Outside, the grounds and outbuildings reflected the light of a full moon. It was like the whole world were a stage and we were waiting for the players to appear. I heard every night sound there was: the barking of the plantation dogs, the screaming of the night bugs, the sound of the hooty owl, some faint singing of spirituals floating up from the negro quarters. I could not sleep, so I lay there inside my mosquito netting and tried to imagine Nat Turner and his men eating barbecue and drinking apple brandy.

Finally I drifted off, only to see flashes of people and scenes behind my eyelids. It was a disturbed and uncomfortable sleep. I thought I felt someone leaning over me. I opened my eyes.

Someone was there.

It was Owen, in the bright light of that Monday morning, August 22, 1831, a day it would take many people a long time to forget.

"Harriet," he said, as if the mere saying of it conveyed everything he was about to tell me. "You've overslept. Get up."

I sat up.

"They're coming. You'd best get up and get dressed."

"Who's coming?" But I knew. When they came for you, you always knew.

"Some people. Nobody knows yet. But they've been riding and attacking and burning and killing all night."

"Killing?"

"Yes. White people. That's their main purpose. They're killing white people. I ran all the way here to tell you. Couldn't find the others. Word has it that they've already killed Travis and his wife, then the people at the Williams plantation. They've hit six homesteads already.

They started with three or five in their band. And now they have a force of fifteen, and nine of them have horses. Come on, get up."

"They're coming here?"

"Yes. Where's Violet? And Margaret? I've got to hide them."

I pulled my blue-and-white-check dress over my head. "She's colored. They won't bother her."

Owen gave me a peculiar look. "Do you know who *they* are, Harriet?"

It had not occurred to me to ask. Nat Turner, of course. But Owen did not know what I knew about Nat. Owen had brought me the warning, but Owen believed that Nat was too good a person to do anything but preach at someone.

"No," I said.

"Nat Turner. He's started an uprising."

"What does that mean?"

"If you stay around you'll find out. Seventeen white people have been killed already."

"How do you know, Owen?" I was sitting on the floor, buttoning my shoes.

"I was with him. Earlier this morning, he asked me to be with him. I stayed until I saw what he was doing.

Harriet, you must run. Into the woods. Go north to the Jacobs place. Warn them. I'll hide Violet."

"And Emilie? And Pleasant? And baby William?" I asked. And my question went on. "And Mother White-head? And Margaret? Where will you hide them all? And Richard? What about Richard?"

"Shut up, Harriet!"

I did as he said.

"Just sneak downstairs and out back and run to the Jacobs place. Somebody has to warn those on the outside."

"Can't I get a horse?"

"No. He's probably got someone stationed in the stable area right now. Just go." He hesitated and looked at me. His eyes went soft and then he did a peculiar thing. "This is in case I never see you again, Harriet."

And he kissed me on the cheek. A brotherly kiss. Tears came to my eyes and it was then and only then that I knew that everything he'd said was true. It was really happening.

I had overslept, so breakfast was already over with. Sleeping late was an unforgivable sin in my house because Richard conducted prayers before breakfast and I'd missed that, too. But this morning no one had come to wake me except Owen. The family was all scattered by now, and the house was eerily silent. They thought they'd done me a good turn by letting me sleep.

I went out the back door. There, just coming into the barnyard, was Nat Turner and his scraggly army of fifteen men, nine of them on horses. Two of them had pine-knot torches still lighted from the night before.

When they leave here, I thought, *they will all be on horses. They will take ours.*

Nat stopped when he saw me. He was not on a horse but walking in front of his men. He held up his hand and they stopped behind him.

"Is this the one what give you trouble, Nat?" one of the men asked. "Let me at her."

"No!" Nat thundered. Then in a softer voice he asked me, "Where is everybody?"

"I don't know."

"You mean you won't tell. Heard about last night already, did you?"

"Nat."

"I thought you were with us. You hated mistreatment of the negro so. You despised what happened on the Gerard plantation. You hate that nincompoop brother of yours. 'S'matter of fact, you pretty much hate everybody. And you gave me the map. I have the key to the gun room, you know."

"You gave it back to Richard."

"You never heard of locksmiths?"

"They wouldn't make a key for a negro."

"When you have a forged letter from a white man they will."

My voice shook. "Did you want to see Richard? I'm sure he's around and will give you whatever it is that you want."

"I want that sly fox of a sister of yours, who's always flirting with me. I want to rip off her blouse and cut her throat. I want that turncoat playmate of yours, that Violet, that half caste who's forgotten she's negro and panders to y'all, just to make life easy for herself. I want that Mother Whitehead with all the rings on her fingers, whose husband left her and who thinks she can buy me at just the blink of one of her blind eyes. I want to give them all their just due."

A catbird cried. The air felt like lead. He was carrying a broadax, not a gun.

"Mother Whitehead's husband died, he didn't run off," I said for lack of anything better to say.

His yellow brown eyes went over me in sadness. "Whatever you want to believe," he said, "before you die."

"Are you going to kill me?"

"I want Richard," he said again. "Where is he?"

One of his men on horseback had ridden a circle around the house and barn and came back to report. "He's in the cotton field with his slaves, boss."

"Well, that's a good place for him to be." Nat started around the barn and his men followed. "I want nobody in the house. Yet," he said. "Hark, grab that little girl and bring her along. I don't want her warning anybody inside. But don't hurt her."

So this was a slave uprising. I'd heard about them all my life, enough to know that plantation owners feared them above flood and fire and insects attacking their crops.

The slave named Hark looked as if he'd lived through ten of them. He personified the very word riffraff, which I'd heard Mother Whitehead use so often, not only about coloreds but about some whites as well.

Hark dragged me along to the cotton field behind the barn and there, sure enough, was Richard, picking cotton with about a dozen slaves. You had to give him that. When there was work to be done, he'd pitch right in and work with the help.

Oh, why hadn't I seen the good things about him before this, and not only the bad?

He looked up as we approached, saw Nat at the head of this devilish tableau, saw me dragged along by Hark, and stopped what he was doing. "What is this?" he said.

Nat stepped forward, at the same time reaching out a muscular arm for one of the pine-knot torches. One man passed it down the line. Nat held it.

"I'm making calls this morning," he told Richard. "We've already visited five plantations and been successfully received. You are number six."

"What do you want?" Richard demanded in his most commanding voice. "And I'll thank you to have that fellow there unhand my sister."

My heart quivered.

"In just a moment," Nat said. "I want her to witness something first."

"What?" Richard said.

Nat handed him the pine-knot torch. "Fire the field," he said.

"What?" Richard was dumbfounded. "Do you know the worth of the cotton in this field?"

"Exactly. And that, preacher man, is why I want you to fire it. Now. Unless you want to see something terrible happen to your sister."

Richard took one look at me and did not hesitate. He accepted the torch, turned, and lighted the cotton. In a minute there was a blaze so high that his servants had to get out of the way.

For me, I thought. *He did it for me.*

Dear God, have I been wrong about everything?

"And now, you spoilt little white girl back there," Nat yelled, "watch this."

And so fast that I did not know what I was supposed to be watching, one of his lieutenants swung his broadax and cut off the top of Richard's head.

I screamed. There was fire and blood everywhere. I pulled away from Hark, screaming and screaming. I picked up my skirts and ran. I expected to be pursued, but no one came.

No one followed. All that followed me was the maniacal laughter from Nat Turner.

Out of the corner of my eye I saw Nat Turner's men whipping out the fire in the cotton field. I thought, *Of course, he doesn't want any neighbors to see the smoke, or they'll come running.*

Then my mental state became tangled again and I couldn't reason.

What had happened? I did not know. I had slept late and Owen was waking me from a nightmare and telling me to run to the Jacobs plantation and invite them for tea.

That is all I could wrap my mind around at the moment. That, and the fact that I must run.

Sixteen

I wasn't used to running. I was accustomed to riding a horse or being taken somewhere in a carriage. I'd ridden many times on this path to the Jacobs place, to convey a message or invitation from Mother Whitehead. But today it was not an ordinary path, not an ordinary ride, not ordinary woods.

I knew that in this wilderness they called Jacobs' Woods, outliers came to hide. Outliers were slaves who'd run off for a week or two to hide out from their masters or mistresses just to show them they objected to certain treatment. To live, they robbed nearby plantations of cattle, sheep, hogs, and tools. Some returned within weeks and proved their point. Others were at large for six months or so. And their owners just waited for them to return.

Owen had been on his way to being an outlier when Nat had caught up with him.

As I ran, stopping every once in a while to catch my breath, I could feel eyes upon me. The outliers were watching, I knew. But they would not concern themselves with me. Likely they already heard what had happened and were hiding now from Nat Turner as well as from their masters.

I fell once and hurt my knee. I tore my dress at the hem. Mother Whitehead would be unhappy, I decided, and I'd get scolded. Then, running, tears coming down my face, I decided that I would likely never see Mother Whitehead again!

Tree branches slapped across my face and I covered my eyes. How long had I been running? My heart was pounding. My head throbbed. There, there up ahead was the Jacobs place. I stopped, so out of breath I thought I would faint. I felt in my dress pocket. Where was the invitation to tea? Had I lost it? Where was my horse? Had he wandered away? Why was I here?

And then it came to me. Somebody had died back home, and I was to tell the Jacobses that if they didn't burn their cotton fields they would die, too.

I stood looking at the back of the Jacobs plantation, at neat fences and cows grazing and horses meandering about. I saw the workers in the field just like at our place. There was an abundance of late summer flowers and there was a pond and there were crisp white curtains at the windows of the crisp white house and a wide veranda and dogs and cats lying about and for a minute I thought I was home.

For a minute I thought I could erase all that had happened this August morning and start over.

Oh, Lord, let me start over. I'll do it right this time. I'll be nicer to Richard. I'll be sorry for my sins. I'll loan Margaret my rose moiré dress that she wanted so. I'll be more patient with Emilie. Lord, try me. Give me a chance.

I closed my eyes, praying. But all I heard was my ragged breath coming in spurts, the tortured beating of my own heart, the barking of the Jacobses' dogs, who had already picked up the scent of me, and the pecking of wood from a nearby woodpecker on a tree.

What I saw behind my closed eyes, though, was different.

I saw five of Nat's men and Nat creeping into the house so quietly that Pleasant, who was upstairs getting William ready for his morning walk, didn't know they were anywhere on the place.

I saw them go onto the veranda in front, where Mother Whitehead had removed herself with Emilie. Violet was up in the attic with Owen, under the bed. Though Mother Whitehead could only see dim shapes and forms, she did see them when they stood in front of her.

"Yes?" she asked. "Who is it? What is it you want? Have you seen Harriet? I want to write some letters. Emilie, who are these people?"

But Emilie was dumbstruck. Her mouth was open but no sound came out. Not even when Hark grabbed her by her hair in back and slit her throat, expertly.

"What's that you say, Emilie?"

Then Nat stepped forward and did his business with the broadax on Mother Whitehead. And, bleeding all over her blue silk morning sacque, Mother Whitehead slumped to the floor dead.

Then they moved out of the room, upstairs to where Pleasant and the baby were. But not before Nat Turner took out his key to the gun room and went to hand weapons to his men who didn't have any guns.

Oh yes, one more thing. There were dead people in the kitchen. Connie for one. She had tried to scream when they forced their way in the door. And two other servants, who had tried to run out. It didn't matter to Nat Turner whether those he killed were black or white, you see. If they sided with the white people, the black people were condemned, too. It was all the same to him. He had his message from God, and he knew what God had told him to do and he would abide by it and earn his way into heaven.

The scene in front of my closed eyes changed now. And I saw Pleasant upstairs in her and Richard's room, leaning over the crib of baby William, cooing him to sleep. I saw Nat Turner and Hark appear in the doorway and take one look around the beautifully appointed blue and white room, with its bed hangings and curtains and dressing table, then, having seen all he wanted to see, Nat gave Hark a shove and Hark stepped across the floor toward Pleasant, who turned and jumped, seeing them. Seeing the broadax in Hark's hands.

She raised her hands to ward them off, but in an instant Hark had swung the broadax and a second later the pristine blue and white of the room had another color added to it. Red. The red blood spilled all over the braided rugs on the

*floor, all down the crib quilt that Pleasant had made for
the baby.*

*She slumped to the floor, near headless now, and baby
William wailed out his anger.*

*Nat Turner told Hark, "Let's go," and Hark said,
"What about the baby?" And Nat said, "Leave him be."
And they started to walk out and then Nat had a change of
heart and stopped at the door. "No," he said, "you're right.
Babies grow up to be men who take revenge. Kill him."*

And so Hark did. And then they left the room.

*I saw all this behind my eyelids, like some madwoman,
within a few seconds. And then I collapsed on the ground.*

Seventeen

"It's all right. It's all right, child. You're safe here. Judd, stop licking her face."

It was Mr. Jacobs's voice. I recognized it from down the years, echoing through some wind of comfort that touched me and dried my tears.

Judd was one of his dogs, a large and, as it turned out, friendly fellow, one of about six that broke away from their restraints to seek me out where I'd been, in the middle of the Jacobses' barnyard, surrounded by clucking chickens and quacking ducks, who marched around me as if they knew what had happened and decided they would protect me.

I didn't know how I'd gotten here, whether I'd walked

or run or crawled through the expanse of field that I was gazing across.

That gave me pause and made me break into a new freshet of crying. That I didn't have complete control of my mind, that it shifted back and forth from the present to the near past. That I could see what had happened with the killings at home as if I'd been there, and knew it all to be true.

"Harriet, are you all right?" Elisha Jacobs was middle sized, well made, intelligent, as well as gentle. When I did not reply, he called, "Emaline! Emaline, come out here, there's something terribly wrong."

He started to stand up straight, but I would not let him. I grabbed onto his arm and subsided my tears enough to get the words out.

"Nat Turner," I hiccuped, "he's risen up against . . . against the white people. He has"—*hiccup*—"about twenty men with him and they've, they've . . ."

"Take your time, child." He knelt next to me.

"They've killed my brother, Richard, and set fire to our cotton fields. Now they're in the house, killing everyone. Ours is . . ."—*hiccup*—"oh Lord, ours is the seventh plantation, and they're coming here next!"

"Emaline, here," and he handed me over to her as she

came running in her long morning gown to fetch me inside, out of harm's way. "Emaline, you and the servants hide down by the springhouse in that gathering of juniper trees. Take care of this child." Then "Fitch!" he called out to his groom. "Get my horse and rifle! I'm riding out to warn the others!"

Still on the dusty ground I asked Mrs. Jacobs, "Can I go with him?"

"No," she said.

Now mounted handsomely on his stallion, Mr. Jacobs leaned down and kissed his wife who had stood up for just the purpose. "No matter what happens, don't come up to the house. Stay down at the springhouse. I don't think they'll fire the house. The flames would give warning to others. Nevertheless, just stay away. I don't want to lose you!"

Then he rode off. Emaline did some calling of her own inside to servants, to assemble some necessities and bring them down to the springhouse.

"Can you walk?" she asked me.

I said yes, I could.

"Fitch," she ordered, "let loose the horses. Open the gate for the cows and the sheep. Let them wander. We'll get them back again." And to me, she said, "Come along,

134

child. I must attend to you. The springhouse is a good place."

I was shaking, both inside and out, as she led the way across the meadow and down the slope and to the springhouse where they, as we did, kept cold the milk and butter and eggs and all other manner of dairy products they produced on their plantation. Somehow I had made this little trip alone, across the field, to their house, unconscious of where I was headed. Now conscious and aided by Mrs. Jacobs and three of her colored servants, all bearing the comforts of home, I could scarce walk.

Their names were Justine, Hope, and Claradine. And, after he was finished with his chores with the animals, Fitch, too, came tagging along, with a rifle, which he apparently knew how to use, from hunting with Mr. Jacobs, I suppose.

And now to protect our lives.

❧

The springhouse was right next to the spring, in a cluster of juniper trees. It seemed protected and peaceful. Claradine had brought along a bundle that turned out to include pillows and blankets, and as soon as we arrived, Mrs. Jacobs, who insisted I call her Emaline, arranged the blanket and pillows and made me lie down. I did so, thinking I'd been lying down already, I was so dizzy and outside of my head.

They had brought some water from the well, some leftover biscuits from breakfast, slices of ham, a hard-boiled egg or two, and apples. We set to eating as if this were a picnic. To Fitch they gave a cold piece of meat on a bone, likely left over from last night's supper, and he gnawed on it, his ever-faithful rifle under one arm.

Emaline, slender, blue-eyed, delicate of hand, pale-skinned and pert-nosed, gave me a powder for my nerves. Then she washed my face and said, "Poor darling, you shall stay with us," and I fell off the cliff I was on and tumbled down into the darkness that had been waiting for me all morning.

I must have had some kind of karma with Nat Turner. I learned that word from Margaret, who learned it in that fancy girls' school she attended. It means you have a spiritual and otherworldly connection with another human being so you know their thoughts and their hopes and ambitions.

I didn't have a whole cloth of karma with Nat, only part. I had sympathized with him, felt his pain, admired his knowledge of God, felt that he had a direct line there. And now, asleep as I was, I saw him and his hellish army approaching the Jacobses' farmyard in their despicable parade of destruction.

I saw the chickens and ducks and goats scatter in their wake, as if no living thing could tolerate it. I saw the few negroes that were about run, and I saw Nat Turner get down off his horse and look around. No, that was our horse, that was Richard's fat white stallion. I saw that many of the others had our horses, too, and our guns. My father's guns. And they still had the pine-knot torches, lighted and at the ready.

I saw all this behind my eyelids, in the blackness that now made up the walls of my soul. Saw them go into that darling wedding cake of a house and do God knows what to Emaline's flowers and chintz sofas and polished furniture, and then, when they could find no one whose head they could slash, they came out, disappointed. But then, to pacify themselves, some were drinking out of whiskey or rum bottles and others were looking ridiculous in Emaline's fancy Sunday go-to-meeting clothes. One had a harmonica and was playing it and they danced a reel, as if at a party. Some were wearing jewels or fancy hats.

Then, at a word from Nat, they stopped. They looked at the house and one handed Nat a torch and then, in a few minutes, a little colored boy of about three came running to them from the barn, his mother running close behind.

One of Nat's helpers slashed him with a sword and left him for dying, and when the mother raised her arms against the man, he slashed her, too. In the same manner that they had slashed Richard. Then they got on their horses and rode off.

"That was Louise and her Izzy," Emaline said dully. "Lord, but she loved that child. I was there when he was born." And she proceeded to cry.

"I'd rather he'd burned the house," she said.

On leaving they had to go through the opening of the white picket fence in front of the house over which Emaline had thrown a few handmade quilts.

I woke up to see the rest. They could have slashed those quilts if all they wanted to do was destroy them. But they didn't.

I sat up and rubbed my eyes in time to see them all get off their horses as if someone had given an order, and then they stood in a row and peed on the quilts.

Fitch asked Emaline if she wanted him to get closer and blow their tails off, but she said no, so he lowered his gun. And then the sordid army, which likely would not even be admitted into hell, remounted their horses and rode away.

Eighteen

I don't rightly know if the words I was saying were coming out the way I wanted them to. Sometimes it seemed to me that they were tumbling about on my tongue and pushing each other around and coming out in no order at all.

I will not deny that I was dazed and befuddled. But I do believe that some of what I said made sense.

In short order I knew I heard a church bell. It sounded, through the thick, hellish August air, slowly and deliberately.

"That's the Blunts," Emaline said. "Theirs is a bell upward of sixty pounds and it can be heard for miles. It usually just rings at mealtimes. But this isn't mealtime, so it must mean that Elisha has gotten there and they are calling for help."

The bell was mournful and steady, and I could have sworn it originated in my heart, but I didn't say anything. We listened to it in near silence for about half an hour, because Emaline said we should wait a while to make sure Turner and his men didn't come back to her place before she headed home.

There was some discussion about me going with her and staying overnight until things settled down.

Did she not know that things would never again be "settled down" for me? Or for anyone touched by today's tragedy?

I said no, I must go home, I had to see what and who I would return to.

By now everyone who had not run, black or white, were likely lying dead. By now even the animals had fled.

Home was the last place in the world I wanted to go. "I must see if anyone is still alive," I said.

"Not yet, child," Emaline told me.

Then, within the next half hour the courier came, a young man on horseback who turned out to be Mr. Blunt's son, John.

He slid from his horse and, without preliminaries, told us of Elisha's arrival and how his father's bell tolling was bringing men from three counties on horseback with guns. "We're ready for Turner," he promised. "Mrs. Jacobs, your husband is anxious for word of you. Do you have a message for him?"

"Tell him I'm going back to the house now," she said. "Tell him Turner has left, most likely on his way to your place. Tell him I love him."

"Yes, ma'am." He mounted his horse and tipped his hat.

"You'd best be careful," Emaline said.

"I will. Thank you, ma'am." And he was across the creek and gone back to his father's plantation. Emaline got to her feet. "No time to waste, let's get on with it," she said. And then, "Harriet?"

For I hadn't risen with the rest of them. Now all stared down at me.

"I can't let you go home yet, child. As the only grown-up around, I feel responsible for you."

"I'll be all right, Emaline. Turner's gone from this direction."

"The devil is never gone," she said. "Elisha won't like it if I let you go home."

"I'll go with her," Fitch guaranteed. "Me an' Bess here." He patted his rifle. "Be back afore you know it, ma'am." You could see the trust between them. Mother Whitehead had trusted Nat Turner that way, too, I thought.

"Servants back at your place who escaped the rampage would care for you," she mused, "but then, how do I know there are any who escaped the rampage? Suppose they are all dead? No, child, you will stay with us until we hear some news, then my husband and I will both escort you home."

She kissed me.

At that moment, as if God were amongst us, Fitch caught sight of two of the Jacobses' horses walking slowly back to the barn. "Ma'am," he said, "I think it's Br'er Rabbit and Br'er Fox come home."

She sighed. "Everybody wants to go home," she said.

We went into the Jacobses' house, which was whole and welcoming and smelled of good things to eat. One of the servants ran a bath for me and helped me scrub the fear and the horror and the disbelief out of myself, and then I told Emaline that I had to write a letter to my uncle Andrew in London. She said yes, do.

She gave me pen and paper. But I couldn't write because I didn't know yet who was dead and who wasn't. So I had a bowl of soup and near fell asleep at the table. Mr. Jacobs came in some time later, and I heard his rumbling voice and felt the dogs next to him as he picked me up and carried me into an upstairs bedroom and put me to bed.

Nineteen

I don't know how long I slept. I don't know if I did right by calling it sleep. I lay with my eyes shut, but my mind never shut down. Is there such a state in the consciousness of people, where they are, for all intents and purposes, asleep, but inside their heads in some place where they don't want to be and can't get out of?

Dreams? I wouldn't dignify them with the name. I saw it all over again behind my closed eyelids, behind flashes of red and white lightning, behind screams and cries for help, what had happened. I saw the flashing broadax that cut the top off Richard's head, felt the feelings of mine that came with it, the impulse to run.

Would this never go away? Would it stay with me forever? And what about what I had *imagined* about the others? Would that stay with me, too? And how much of it was true?

Once, I got up out of bed and went to sit in a nearby chair, just to test my own aliveness, to see if I were really not at home, and if this were truly the Jacobs place.

Then I got back into bed, shivering. I preferred to be awake. I could command away my thoughts, concentrate on the present. I could think on what time of year this was and what had to be done on the farm. I knew because I had copied it down in so many of Mother White-head's letters.

It would soon be September. *Sept. 1 thru 17—plough in the stubble of the first wheat field and sow buckwheat, 40 acres in 13 ploughing days.*

The hands must start soon! I got up out of bed. Who would tell them to start? Was anyone left to tell them? Were there any hands left?

I dressed quickly and parted the curtains. It was daylight outside. I went downstairs.

❧

It was near noon on the third day of my stay at the Jacobses'. We were at the midday meal in the dining room.

They fussed over me. I assured them I was all right but about starved, and Claradine fetched me a plate of food from the kitchen. I felt it a betrayal to be so hungry and to eat so unashamedly, but nobody said anything.

Mr. Jacobs put down his coffee cup and cleared his throat. "I've been over to your place twice already," he said to me.

I stopped eating.

He stirred his coffee. "Took help with me. I'm sorry to have to tell you, Harriet, but they're all dead. All except some of the hands who hid out, and the kitchen help."

My eyes went wide. "Mother Whitehead and Pleasant?"

"Sorry, child."

"Baby William? And Violet and Owen?"

"Baby William. But not Violet and Owen. They hid out, too. The first time I went back, I and the servants and hands buried everyone in the family burying ground. Oh yes, we buried that little girl, too. Emilie."

She'd been visiting. I started to cry, silent tears running down my face.

"The servants agreed to clean up the place. They said they'd do that yesterday."

"Harriet," Emaline put in, "do you think you should go back there? Mayhap you should stay with us a while."

For an answer I broke into tears. Emaline came to me and bent over and put her arms around my shoulders, and I allowed her to comfort me. "I must go back," I said. "I'm the one the place belongs to now. And Violet and Owen will be looking for me. They all will."

"Of course," she said. "But just stay this day. Give the servants one more day to make the place fit for human habitation."

When we got home, it was the first time in my life that I realized the house where you grew up had a grip on you that it had no right to keep. That you didn't really have had to be happy there for it to claim this hold. And that this would be true and lasting even if I never went inside that house again.

Something sinister about the house would stand, tall and sprawling inside my soul, its beams supporting all my fears, its windows allowing me to peer out at the world with a dark view I could never lose, its veranda giving me a place to sit and argue with my childish ideals.

When that distressful thought seized me, as I sat astride Br'er Fox, while Mr. Jacobs dismounted and looked around, I was completely defeated. I could always and forever stay away, but this white and now-ghostly place would always be with me, so familiar that every time I saw a plantation house with ceiling-to-floor windows and two chimneys on top it would bring back the whole texture of my childhood.

"Where is everyone?" I asked Mr. Jacobs.

Then, from inside, came a familiar voice and my heart leaped up in my throat.

"Here we are, Harriet. Safe as two pups at their mother's breast."

It was Violet. She came with Owen out the back door and across the porch and down the steps to greet us.

"You"—oh, I could not think of words to call them—"y'all are such old mean things to do this to me, to play tricks on me now that I'm home. I was so scared."

There were hugs and tears all around, and then came the servants from the kitchen, just as I'd last seen them, Connie and Ormond, Henry Jack, Charlotte, and Winefred.

Connie! In my fevered imagination I'd seen her killed by Turner's men. I was so glad now that all my imaginings weren't true.

Nine other servants, besides the field workers, were

saved. Owen counted on his fingers. "Walley and his wife, Mariah, Cyrus, Daniel, Gowrie, Bryan, Herbert, Gideon, and Ralph. All of them helped us clean up the bodies and wrap them in sheets. Mr. Jacobs, here, supervised. We buried them in the small family cemetery under the juniper tree. We put Richard there, too."

"We should get Mr. Jacobs some food and tea and let him start on his way home," I said.

"I'll take care of that," Connie offered, and she led Mr. Jacobs into the kitchen.

I put a hand on Owen's arm. "You knew him. Did you ever think?"

"No." There were tears in the corners of his eyes. "He was such a good man. No one can believe what he's done. I won't even let myself think about it now."

It came to me, as I followed them, as I finally entered the house, that I was entering as someone else, not as the Harriet I had been before. She was a stranger, a transient, gone. I allowed myself to be pleasantly surprised by things I scarce noticed before: the knitted afghans that Mother Whitehead had made, the boxed geraniums outside the windows, the summer organdy curtains that I knew must soon be taken down, the Persian carpets, and the piano over there in the corner.

Blind as she was, Mother Whitehead had played beautifully.

I drew myself up straight. I knew that I must take charge and run things, and that if I did that, I must take on the manner of Mother Whitehead. One who was in charge possessed certain qualities.

I went, first, into the kitchen and sat at the table with Mr. Jacobs, to see that he was properly taken care of, that he had the best slices of ham, that his bread was fresh, and likewise the fruit. That the tea was freshly brewed. Before it was time for him to go on his way, I directed Owen to see to it that his horse was given food and water and brushed down, and I accompanied him outside to see him off and to thank him, assuring him that soon I would have him and Emaline over for dinner.

Then I went inside my house.

Violet and Owen followed me everywhere, as if I needed guarding.

I went into the parlor, drew in my breath, and looked around. It was chilly, for the afternoon sun had not yet made its presence known here.

"Have Ormond light a fire," I directed. "I will have tea and refreshments here."

Owen scrambled to do my bidding.

Violet asked me what she could do. I took her hand. "Keep me company," I said. "Don't leave me alone unless I tell you. Talk to me."

So she told me how my sister, Margaret, was the only one in all the killings that Nat Turner had killed himself.

"He was in love with Margaret," I said. "And he couldn't have her. So he killed her."

I could run this place. Why not? I knew what was in all Mother Whitehead's letters, who her suppliers were, whom Richard did business with. He had it all in his account books.

Yes, I decided. I would run the place. "And after tea I will have paper and pen. I must write a letter," I told her.

"Yes, Miss Harriet." Her manner had changed toward me. She was picking up on my lead. She saw what I was trying to do.

So after tea and scones, she brought me the necessary things and I wrote my letter.

Dear Uncle Andrew: I wish you would come and visit me. Everyone here is dead.

Your loving niece, Harriet Whitehead

Twenty

"**I** was in the attic. With Owen. Under the bed," Violet told me. "I didn't see it. Please, Harriet, ask someone else. I can't talk about what I did see." Tears were coming down her face and she wiped them away with her hand.

"I don't want someone else. You're my closest friend. I want to hear it from you."

She sat on the floor, at my feet. She hesitated only a moment and then the words came, or rather tumbled, off her tongue.

"Like I said, Owen grabbed me the minute we saw them coming into the house. Somehow he knew that Nat had turned into a crazy man and wasn't the Nat who had helped him in the past. 'There's a place in him I hoped he'd never go,' he told me. 'I sensed it all the time. Like he was teetering on a ledge and deciding whether to jump. And now he's jumped, Violet. So let's get out of here.'

"I suggested my room upstairs. Few people even know there's an attic in the house. But for safekeeping we went under the bed. All we could hear were voices and screams from below stairs. We both knew your brother, Richard, was already dead. And we knew he was killing Mother Whitehead and Emilie. Out the window we could see the cotton field burning and some slaves trying to put the fire out.

"Then Owen said we should take the servants' stairs down and see what we could do. It was chancy, but a good idea. Besides, Pleasant was on the second floor with baby William. Maybe we could help her."

"But they killed Pleasant," I objected. "At least in my head they did."

She nodded her head very vigorously. "We crept down the servants' stairway and peeked through the door, just a crack. Turner was there in the hall with one of his henchmen, who had his sword drawn, and Pleasant was facing them. 'Kill me if you wish,' she was saying, 'you've already killed my husband. And he was good to you. You might as well kill me, too.'

"So," and here Violet gulped some air and continued, "the henchman did. Right there in the hall. Then Turner looked around asking for Margaret. He wanted Margaret real bad, like. He was ready to gather his men and leave, and then the baby cried from the bedroom."

There was a moment's silence. I heard the tolling of more than one church bell now, and we waited, listening. So different from my imaginings, but no less cruel. Then Violet continued.

"Somebody said, 'What about the baby?' At first Nat said, 'Never mind,' then he changed his mind and said, 'No, we must get the baby, too. Babies grow up and take revenge.' And then he and one man went into where the baby was, and from where Owen and I were hiding, we dared not move or talk or even breathe, but we heard baby William's screams, and then silence.

"Then they left. I'm so sorry, Harriet. We should have done something about baby William."

"There was nothing you could do," I told her.

I sat, studying on the whole thing. But I could not wrap my mind around it. It was too terrible, too out of my circle of possibilities. "I don't think anything like this has ever happened before in Virginia," I told her.

She nodded her assent. "Owen said he heard that fifty-seven people were killed."

"What was he trying to do? What did he want?"

"I don't know. I think he wanted to capture Jerusalem. That's what all the servants are saying. And collect an army and kill some more."

"And now?"

"Now they're hunting him. We should pray they catch him."

I had a thought then. "Did he attack the Gerard place?"

"Yes," she said. "Everybody over there is dead."

I did not ask how she knew. The negro grapevine traveled faster than the wind. My tears wouldn't come and my mouth was dry. "Could I have another cup of tea?" I asked.

Apparently a few servants had been standing in the hall, outside the parlor, listening to Violet's recitation.

"I'll get the tea, mistress," Connie said.

"She called me mistress," I whispered to Violet.

"Yes, you are mistress now of this plantation," she said.

"I'm not even mistress of myself," I thought aloud.

155

"But I know I can do it." I smiled at Violet. "Do you think I can do it?" I asked.

"We'll all help you. Everybody has their job and knows how to do it. And for anything else you want, you must assign the tasks. Tell us what it is that you wish us to do."

That afternoon I held a meeting in the kitchen. It had started to rain outside and that seemed fitting. Everyone crowded around.

"I want Walley to be the overseer, as I heard Richard say one time he would be a good one. And I want you to take over with the house, Winefred. Connie is to be the cook. And Ormond knows what his job is. Owen, you are to help Ormond and answer doors and keep him supplied with wood for the hearths, just as you've been doing. And I want you to tell me now, Violet, what happened to Cloanna?"

"She's alive," Violet said. "Turner never went to the quarters."

"Then you must visit her as soon as you can. Bring her a side of ham and some small beer. As for work, it must go on. The rest of the cotton has to be picked and bundled and shipped. The apples, too. The animals must be cared for. *And we must plough in the stubble of the first wheat field and sow buckwheat, forty acres in thirteen ploughing days."*

Walley looked hard at me. "Where did you get that from, miss?"

I raised my chin. "I learned from writing Mother Whitehead's letters. I must contact her cotton factors, Jenkins, Middleton, and Pierce, and set a date for the cotton to be delivered, too. We must get our heads together on that date, Walley."

"Yes, miss."

"You see," Violet said to me later when we were alone, "you make a fine mistress."

When I wasn't being "mistress" I sat in Mother Whitehead's chair in the parlor for days, it seemed. I could not move. I did not want to speak to anyone. I just wanted to stare out the ceiling-to-floor windows through the leaden air of the last days of that August and adjust my mind to the new world I had been dragged into, screaming.

One morning Ormond was wiping off the glass panes of the lower parts of the windows in the parlor, for the dogs were kept inside now at my request. They were good watchdogs, but their nose prints were on the glass panes.

I had always wanted them in the house. Mother Whitehead would never allow it. They were of the large type, with loud barks, and I felt safer with them around me. They slept at my feet, days, and by my bedside, nights, and were alert to every noise. They were clean and devoted. Punch and Judy, their names were. And that's what Ormond was doing that morning. Cleaning the windowpanes in the parlor.

"Did they mess the windows again?" I asked.

"It's all right, Miss Harriet. They give you comfort."

"What's that on the rag? Blood?"

He looked at the rag in his hands. "Yes, miss, from the bottom windowpane."

I understood immediately, as I understood his discomfort. "From that day?" I asked.

"Yes, miss. Left on the window. I must have missed it the last time I . . ."

"It's all right, Ormond. It is, truly."

Blood on the corner of a windowpane, from the day Mother Whitehead was killed. Would the memories ever be cleaned out of this house? Out of our minds?

Already they were in print in all the newspapers in the East. Already all the rumors that had circulated that day were being put to rest. That the British were attacking, that there were piles of dead children's bodies being buried in a common grave near Jerusalem. That Governor John Floyd received word there was an insurrection in Richmond, that one slave who refused to join Nat's army had his heel strings cut so he couldn't run and alert anybody.

And soon, following those articles and the rumors, would come the investigations, Violet and Owen told me.

And my initials were on that map. Nat Turner was still running free. I tried not to think about all that, although I did worry the matter about Nat Turner still being free.

Would he come back here? The idea took hold of me and I became frightened. When I told Connie and Winefred and Ormond about it, they suggested we put a trundle bed in my room and have Violet sleep with me.

I liked that idea. Why hadn't I thought of it? Then I had another. I knew that Ormond used to hunt with Richard and, therefore, knew how to use a gun. So we purchased new firearms and I asked him to arm whatever negroes he thought trustworthy and teach them to shoot. Because I was still frightened.

It was a big step, but hadn't I heard that faithful ne-groes on the attacked plantations had fought back at Nat Turner's army and some had driven them away?

Things had changed. We must change with them, I decided. We must be prepared.

Twenty-One

A week, and then two, went by. News from the outside came to us, from the post carrier, the newspapers, the slave grapevine, and Emaline, who, true to her word, came to supper one night with her husband. Was it proper to entertain so soon after such a tragedy? There were no rules in the books for it. There were no books for it in the first place.

What would they say? *It is advisable, socially, to wait at least a month to serve beef and roasted potatoes and peas from the garden after your brother has had the top of his head slashed off as the result of a slave revolt.*

"That Nat Turner hasn't been captured yet," Emaline told us. "They had him for a couple of hours at the Black

ANN RINALDI

Head Sign Post, but he got away. Someone saw him at the Travis place, and the Isle of Wight County Militia went after him, but he was nowhere to be found."

I shivered. We were having dessert.

"It's fearful that he's still out there somewhere, isn't it?" she asked.

"I have my dogs," I told her. "And now all the male negroes on this place know how to use a gun."

"You know what they are saying about Turner's up-rising?" she asked me. "They are saying that the faithful blacks on the plantations whipped him more than the whites did. Why, the blacks were on the verandas and behind trees and on rooftops, firing away at Turner and his men. Nat Turner didn't expect that. He expected all the bound servants to join him. But if not for them, he might have taken Jerusalem. He was within a mile of it, they say."

When she left, she kissed me and told me not to be a stranger. "After all," she said, "you were the one who alerted everyone. If not for you . . ." and she shook her head and sighed. "You were our female Paul Revere that day. We owe our lives to you, Harriet Whitehead."

I blushed and said, "Thank you. I was out of my head."

And she said, "Oh blather, you knew what you were doing. And let me know when your uncle Andrew arrives. We'll have you both over to dinner."

♪

The Virginia Militia came to our place the third week Nat Turner was not yet captured and Ormond ushered their commander, a Lieutenant Berry, into the parlor to see me.

"Are *you* the mistress of this place?" he asked me.

"Yes. Everybody else is dead."

"I'd heard that the Reverend Whitehead was killed in the rebellion."

"Yes. His head was slashed. I am the only member of the family to survive. What can I help you with, Lieutenant?"

"We have orders, miss, to search the quarters of all the slaves and free blacks. We're looking for scattered powder and shot, to make sure they weren't involved in the insurrection."

I sighed. *You should be searching my quarters,* I told myself. I called out for Violet and she came. I introduced her.

"Are you free or bound?" the lieutenant asked her.

"She's bound. For now," I said. "I have not yet had time to think about the future."

He nodded. "Pardon me, miss, but you seem awfully young to be making such decisions."

"My uncle Andrew is, at this very moment, on a ship coming from London," I recited. And that pacified him. I also said that Violet would accompany him and his men on rounds, that he was not to upset old Cloanna in her quarters, and that he was to check in with me before he left.

I had heard, you see, of this man and his militia, and how they went on some plantations and planted false evidence to implicate some slaves, and then arrested them and took them away. Just to make it seem as if they were doing something. Because, with Nat Turner still at large, it seemed as if nobody was doing anything at all.

Lieutenant Berry was polite, a true Southerner, if nothing else. He bowed. He saluted. He even kissed my hand. I thought how jealous my sister, Margaret, would be. And then I felt a pang of guilt.

I must, this very afternoon, find out the particulars of her death.

Twenty-Two

The appearance of the militia at our plantation frightened me.

What would happen when Nat Turner was caught? Would they go through his possessions? Would they find the map with my initials on it? Oh God, I prayed, don't let them go through his things until I can see him.

For if I was the Paul Revere who had saved them all with my warning, I was surely also the Benedict Arnold who had betrayed them all to begin with.

I had every intention of asking Violet and Owen about Margaret's death that afternoon. And I knew what they had to tell me was bad. Nightmare fodder. The stuff of hauntings. Because, since I'd been home, both of them had never quite been able to look me straight in the eye. And whenever Margaret's name came up, as it often did, they either gave the subject a new turn, or excused themselves and left the room.

I now took all my meals at a small side table in the parlor. I could not bear to sit alone at the long, polished table in the dining room with the crystal chandelier dripping its blessing down on me. The chairs and place settings for the family were all there, and I tried, a few times, to sit in my place, but I could not eat for seeing Richard at the head of the table and Mother Whitehead to his right.

So I started eating in the parlor. Sometimes before a glowing fire in the hearth, now that October had come.

October. I should be at my lessons. But that would remind me too much of Pleasant, so I didn't go near my schoolbooks. I read for my own pleasure.

Owen kept the fires going for me, and hovered near, keeping a conversation going.

It was Owen then, who told me about the last of the flowers in the small garden to the right of the house, a sort of horseshoe-type garden.

"Sad to see the last of the flowers," he said.

"I'll visit them right after lunch," I told him.

And I did. And that's how I found out how Margaret died.

∽◦◦

Punch and Judy were tagging after me. The weeds were high in the garden. I must assign someone to pull them. I had never been much on flowers. It was one of Mother Whitehead's complaints about me, and when she wished to punish me for something, she'd send me out here to pull weeds, or lug water in a watering can from the well to water them. Red, blue, or yellow, I didn't know their names.

"You disgrace yourself," she'd told me. "All proper Southern girls know and love flowers."

I was thinking of having Violet pick a bouquet of those purple and pink ones in the far corner when Judy came over to me with a fat stick in her mouth. She was whimpering, as she did when she was especially proud of herself and wanted praise.

"What is it?" I asked her.

She dropped the stick at my feet.

It was actually more than a stick. It was as round and fat as a man's upper arm, and what was that all over it?

It was blood, that's what it was. All over it.

I bent down and picked it up. It was rather heavy. I held it in both hands and brought it into the house, into the parlor where I sat and read of an afternoon, where the fire crackled and I took tea, where I was mistress, and where I could seal out all bad memories.

I called for Violet and Owen.

Owen saw what lay on the Persian carpet between us and looked down at it, shamefaced. "I should have gotten rid of it," he said.

"I thought you did," said Violet.

They spoke of the piece of wood as if it was a murder weapon, which indeed, it was.

"Is this what killed Margaret?" My voice was low, but somehow I couldn't make it any louder.

"No," Owen said.

"Yes," said Violet.

I looked from one face to the other. "Well, which is it? Tell me."

Owen did the telling:

"We were behind the door of the servants' stairway and we could hear and see what was going on down here. They had just killed Mother Whitehead and Emilie. Then they killed Pleasant, who'd come down upon hearing the commotion, and then they went upstairs to baby William. When Nat came down after Hark killed baby William, he asked for Margaret. Where was she?

"She'd run outside to hide in the garden. Violet and I were in the attic again by then, and we looked out the window down on the garden. Margaret was hiding behind the rose trellis and he'd come out looking for her. He was holding a long sword he got from your father's gun room.

"He saw her and started chasing her. She ran and ran in that garden, from the rose trellis to the pussy willow tree to the zinnia patch and then she slipped and fell and he, he . . . he slashed her with his sword.

"But she didn't die immediately. She wouldn't cooperate. And I saw him leaning over and patting her head and then, of a sudden, he picks up this piece of wood and raises it high and slams it down on her head, how many times I don't know, but enough to kill her. Then he leaves her there and takes off with his men around back. To get some horses, I suppose. Because everyone else he wanted to kill was dead.

"I wanted . . . I wanted to go down and stop him, but Violet said he'd kill me, too. I had no weapons, and all his men were downstairs, looting and drinking.

"And then I heard, after it was all over, that fifty-seven were killed in the uprising, but that Margaret was the only one Nat Turner killed himself. He killed no other."

I nodded my head. "Thank you, Owen. Now if you could burn this log."

He picked it up and started toward the hearth.

"No," I said. "No. Not in here. Take it outside and burn it. Please."

He did as I said. I was left with Violet.

"I couldn't let him go down and try to rescue her, Harriet," she told me. "Nat's men would have killed him in a minute."

"Fifty-seven dead," I said dully, "and Margaret the only one he killed himself."

"Yes," she said.

"I wonder, did he love her that much?"

"The servants all say he—" and she stopped there.

"Yes, Violet, tell me."

"They say he lusted after her."

I sighed. I was not surprised. Margaret had sashayed around in front of him every time he was here. So he personally punished her the only way he could. He killed her.

"I have a headache, Violet," I said. "Would you get me a powder and some water?"

She fetched it. She gave me the powder and water and I lay back on the divan and she covered me with an afghan that Mother Whitehead had crocheted. "You must promise," I said, gripping her wrist, "to tell me the minute Nat Turner is captured."

She said she would, and I fell asleep and dreamed of running through the garden and hiding behind the rose trellis with Nat Turner in pursuit.

Twenty-Three

As the fall deepened, as the leaves turned on the trees and the flowers died and the crops were brought in, as the cotton was baled and shipped out to Jenkins, Middleton, and Pierce, as the farm potatoes were harvested and the peas stored in the barn to dry, more and more places were found in the house where there were bloodstains.

Carpets, backs of chairs, upholstery, and corners of bedspreads all had to be repaired or thrown out. And then, of course, there was a great deal of ordering to do. I wrote twice to the cotton factors to send to England for carpets and bedspreads, not to mention items we could not grow or manufacture here or in Jerusalem like molasses, sugar, paints, certain fabrics, and the chairs I wanted. After all, this was my place now. A little newness, a few different touches might distract me from what had happened.

Then once I started, and with Violet's help, I went over the books, I saw that the profits the fall crops had yielded were above what we had expected, mayhap because so many of the plantations around us had been destroyed and there was nobody to bring in those crops.

For a while I felt guilty, as if I were making a profit on the misfortune of others. But then I decided that we'd had enough misfortune for God to forgive me for any profit I made. And that our crops were needed to feed the hungry around us this winter.

To get back to my purchases: I decided that the downstairs hallway carpet, which had been mud splattered that terrible day, and since cleaned, should be replaced.

I ordered a Persian carpet from London, along with some blue-and-white-flowered drapes for the front parlor. I would spend most of my time there in the winter. It would be a grave sin not to brighten it up.

I was sitting in that parlor with the account books on my lap, wondering what Mother Whitehead and Richard would say about my extravagances, when both Violet and Owen came in to see me. I looked up.

"They caught Nat Turner," Violet said.

I near dropped the account book from my lap. "Where?"

"Near the Travis place, where he started out. He built a cave there and lived in it after his slave army broke up. He came out at night," Owen reported. "Other slaves brought him food they stole from the Travis plantation."

I drew in my breath. "Is he in jail now?"

"Yes," they said in unison.

"Did they find any papers on him?"

"You're thinking of the map, aren't you?" Violet asked.

I nodded.

"He had no papers on him from what I've heard," Owen said.

"He must have left them in the cave, if he didn't lose them," Violet allowed.

We just looked at one another, the three of us. Nobody spoke. It wasn't necessary. And then it came to me for the first time in the weeks since the killings that something else wasn't necessary, either. It wasn't necessary for me to ask anybody's permission for what I wanted to do.

There was nobody to account to anymore. And I felt free and a little scared, all at the same time.

⟨∽⟩

We took horses, because the day was half spent already and, while not a great distance away, it was no hop, skip, and jump, either, to the Travis place. It was the beginning of November now and the leaves were gone from the trees and naked tree branches danced against a hard blue sky and piles of leaves blew in the wind.

My soul was attuned to what we were going to do. We were on a subversive mission, and the weather was in tune with it.

Did anybody know where the cave was, besides the authorities? We rode hard and the horses seemed glad of it. The wind tousled my hair and I seemed one with it, as if I were working off all my grief and despair. And soon we got to the Travis place.

Should we knock on the door? The place was deserted, with the exception of a few chickens clucking in the barnyard.

What did we expect? We'd heard the story. This was the place Nat had come from, the people from whom

Mother Whitehead had gotten him on loan. And it was the first plantation he'd struck at in his uprising.

He and his men had stopped here for some cider. It had been given to them by the slave Austin. The Travis family had gone to late church services and not gotten home until midnight. They had gone to sleep immediately and were indeed sleeping as Hark secured a ladder and set it against a second-floor window.

Nat went into the room of his sleeping master and hit Travis in the head with his hatchet, but the blow didn't kill him. One of his men finished Travis off. Then the man turned his ax on Sally, Travis's wife, and killed her.

Then the children, including the little baby sleeping in the cradle. They then went downstairs, taking four guns, a few old rifles, and gunpowder, and went on to the next plantation, that of Salathul Francis, six hundred yards away.

So no, we wouldn't knock on the Travis door. We might wake the ghosts.

We wandered over to the empty barn, and there we met a wandering, dazed slave. Was this Austin? We said hello. He nodded.

"Do you know where Nat Turner's cave is?" we asked him.

"I never give him no vittles when he wuz dere," he told us.

"We're not saying you did," Owen said. "But do you just know where it is? We'd like to see it, is all, before all the other people come by to stare at it."

He took us to it. He asked no other questions. He told us he was living on the Travis place because he had nowhere else to go. He was eating the corn from the field. He had already eaten the ham and the chicken in the house. "Soon," he said, "soon there be no more food and Austin die."

"You come over to us, Austin," I said. "You can work for me. I can use you. I'll give you food and shelter."

He just stared at me, a little girl by all standards, offering him a job. Did he even know who I was?

"I'm Harriet Whitehead," I told him. "My whole family was killed by Nat Turner, but our plantation still is working and I could use your help."

"Yes, ma'am," he said in a singsongy way. "I be there. I come."

❧

We tethered our horses on a fence and walked to the cave, which was just on the edge of the woods that circled the plantation on two sides. It was hidden by some poplar trees and covered with the branches of evergreens so that, coming upon it, you could never tell it was there.

"There 'tis," Austin said proudly, as if the whole thing was his idea to begin with, his creation. "You all want Austin to wait?"

"No, Austin," I said. "What I would like you to do is give our horses some water. Are you good with horses?"

"Austin wuz the master's groom," he said.

"Good. I have a groom. But I need another man in the stable. Why don't you do that, then gather your things and start over to our place. Ask for Walley, the overseer. Tell him what I said about you and that we'll be home before supper."

He left us, and we started removing the evergreen boughs from the opening of the cave. It was not a small affair. A person could fit into the opening without bending over. All it lacked was light. But a few minutes after we went inside, my eyes adjusted to the dimness enough for me to see that there were, amongst other things, two lanterns.

"I wish I had a lucifer match," I said.

"Here, I have one," Owen offered.

"Owen," I said in mock surprise, "do you smoke?"

He did not answer, just picked up the lanterns and lighted them, gave one to me and kept one himself. They cast eerie light in the cave.

If I had time, I would be squeamish. If I had time, I would be scared. But I did not have time for such childish emotions anymore. Not after what I'd seen and been told about.

With the lantern light we could make things out. "There's extra clothing," I said. "Someone must have brought it for him. And pillows and blankets."

"What's this?" Violet picked up a book. "Why, it's a Bible!"

"Look for a folder or something that he would keep papers in," I urged.

We searched the far, dank corners of the cave, and finally I found it. A portfolio-type leather folder, such as the kind Richard used to carry. Inside it were papers. I gave my lantern to Violet and she held it high over the papers. There were notes about the plantations they'd "done," the people they'd "finished," and, then, then, finally, there was the map.

The map I'd traced for him. On paper Pleasant had given me. The map of Southampton County. Without which he could not have found his way around to all the farms. Without which he could not have killed all those people. And children.

But because of me, and my childish fancies, he had it. Because he preached about a God who loved us and forgave us. And Richard preached about an angry God, a punishing God. What kind of God, I wondered, was awaiting Nat Turner now?

The map had notes all over it, in Nat Turner's small, neat writing. And down in the right-hand corner it had my initials. H.W.

"Oh God," I prayed. "Oh God, thank you."

Twenty-Four

We came home at dusk, the sweetest part of the day on the plantation. Candles were lighted in all the windows, and I felt that the old home was trying to be itself and just might yet be restored to what it had been after all.

We took the horses to the barn and Chancy, the groom, took charge of them.

"Look at what we look like," Violet said. "We'll catch the devil for sure."

"Isn't anybody to hand it out to us," I said, brushing off my skirt front. To be sure, we were full of dust and grime. Richard would have had apoplexy and likely sent me to my room to reflect on my sins.

"Is my face dirty?" I asked Violet.

"It's all smudged. I suppose mine is, too."

I nodded. At that precise moment a bell tolled in the distance. Seven tolls. Well, we weren't too late for supper. And then, as we were standing on the back porch in the semidarkness, the door opened, spilling light onto us.

Ormond stood there. "Miss Harriet, you have company. You'd best come in now."

Company? I cast a quick look down at myself. My shoes were muddy, my hair all straggly, and in one hand I still clutched the rolled-up map of Nat Turner's with my initials on it.

"Who, Ormond? Who is it? Do I have time to change?" Someone wanting to interview me about Nat Turner perhaps. I'd had two such someones in the last month. One from the *Richmond Enquirer* newspaper and another from the *Alexandria Gazette*.

"Why it's your uncle, Miss Harriet. Your uncle Andrew. You've been expecting him, haven't you? He arrived an hour ago. He's in your brother's library. Waiting."

Uncle Andrew! I'd forgotten all about him. Did he still exist? He was from a time of life that I'd labeled "before," wasn't he? Before the rebellion.

Without realizing it, I'd made file drawers in my head

and put certain people in them. Some who'd been killed in the rebellion were in locked drawers, others were in drawers that were half open, meaning they could still be talked about.

Uncle Andrew was in a drawer I'd left open by mistake. I'd invited him, I recollected, asking him to come, right after the uprising, telling him that everyone here was dead. And he'd settled his business in London, gotten passage, likely on one of my father's steamers, and come.

And I'd forgotten he was making the long journey. I hadn't even planned a room for his comfort.

"Violet," I said, "do something."

"What would you have me do, Harriet? Just tell me."

"Richard and Pleasant's old bedroom. I know it's clean. See to it that there are fresh sheets on the bed and a fire in the hearth and candles in the windows. Sprinkle some lavender around."

"It's already been done, Miss Harriet," Ormond intoned. "I've seen to it. I've settled him into the room. I was sure you'd want that room for him since it's the most commodious one in the house."

"Ormond, you're a treasure. Do you think I've time to change?"

He shook his head slowly. "I think it best if you present yourself now. I've been entertaining him for the last hour, and your brother's best rum is near gone. I told him I didn't know where you all were . . . because," he said, obviously put out about the whole thing, "I didn't, Miss Harriet. Nobody told me. Or any of us. Winefred held supper. Now you'd best get on in there and you'd best use all your charm. He is growing impatient. And worried. What kind of place is this, he's about to ask, that nobody knows where the little mistress is? Go now. Quick."

"Thank you, Ormond." I gave him a quick hug as I went into the house.

He was seated behind the oak desk that Richard had loved so. He was going over the ledgers that told of the profits and the losses of the plantation. He was sipping some rum.

I stood in the doorway. "Uncle Andrew?"

He looked up. I hadn't thought of him as tall or as having a full head of hair or as wearing spectacles. He had a long nose and piercing eyes, and yet somehow everything fused together to make him not handsome, but striking. A man of consequence.

"Harriet?"

He stood up and came forward. "Child? Is it you? The writer of all those letters? Why I came as fast as I could when you wrote, 'everyone here is dead.'" He held out his arms and I went to him.

He enfolded me in those arms so tightly that the hug said things both of us hadn't even thought of yet. He patted the top of my head. "I've been here over an hour, child. Where have you *been*? All the servants were worried about you."

I had a lie all ready. I was going to say I and Violet and Owen had been out searching for a lost colt, but something told me that lies had no legs around this man. Besides, it was good to have someone ask me where I'd been with such real concern.

I drew back from him. I was still holding the map of Southampton County. "I went to find Nat Turner's cave," I said. "Did anyone here tell you the story about what happened?"

"They didn't have to. It was in all our papers abroad. What a god-awful shame. And you knew this man? He worked here?"

"Yessir."

"And you went to get his *map,* you say?"

"Yes, Uncle."

He stepped back a bit, his hands on my shoulders. "So that's why you look as if the cat just dragged you in. You've been in his cave. Alone?"

"No, sir, my girl, Violet, and our houseboy, Owen, came with me. I had to find the map, you see."

"No, I confess, I don't." He had an English accent and I enjoyed hearing it. "Suppose you tell me."

It came to me then that he was asking for an explanation. And that I must answer to him. That he was in charge now and a mite less than happy with my tardiness and my appearance.

"It's a long story, sir, and they're waiting supper."

"They've held it up for an hour, at least, they can wait ten minutes more."

So I told him then how I'd drawn, or rather traced, the map for Nat Turner. How, out of pride, I'd initialed my name in the bottom corner. How he'd told me he was going plantation to plantation to preach, after the public whipping at the Gerard plantation. How he was known as a preacher and I'd never known him to be anything but gentle and kind. I was shamefaced when I was finished. There were tears in the tone of my voice.

I showed him the map. He spread it out on the desk

and examined it carefully, especially the notes Nat Turner had made. Then he looked at me.

"The authorities are going to want this map," he said.

"Please, Uncle," I begged. "That's why I went to get it. Please, I can't let them know I gave it to Nat Turner. Even though I didn't know what he was going to do. I can't let people, in years to come, see my initials on it. Please."

He sat looking at me steadily. "I see you've thought this through."

I nodded yes.

"What were you going to do? Destroy it?"

I said, yessir, I was.

"We can't do that," he admonished. "We must give it over to the authorities."

Tears welled in my eyes and started down my face.

"I've always prided myself on being an honest man," he said quietly. "And now I'm home. And in charge. And head of the plantation. And I must decide what to do."

I sniffed and nodded.

He took out his handkerchief and wiped my face. "Tell you what, though, I haven't *always* been that honest. I couldn't, though I wanted to be. I've lied to you all these months and months, for one thing. Which was a bad thing to do. So, to make up for it, to you, what say I just erase these initials you put on the bottom corner here and then we turn the map over to the authorities? What do you say, hey, Harriet?"

And all the time, there he was, carefully erasing my initials off the map. I just stared at him. My mind was unable to wrap around it all yet. What was it he had said? Why was he erasing my initials? Because he'd *lied* to me? When? About what?

I asked him then. "What did you lie to me about all these months, sir?"

He pushed the map aside. "Something very important, Harriet," he said. "You see, I'm not your uncle. I'm your father."

Twenty-Five

One would think that after what I'd seen of late, after what my eyes had been shown and what my ears had been forced to listen to and my tongue had had to say and been unable to say, that nothing would take me aback anymore.

My father.

I just stared at the man. The word found no familiar place to rest in my brain.

"My father is dead, sir," I told him. "Been dead all these years. Are you an impostor then? Shall I call Owen and Ormond and have them put you off the place?"

He laughed. He got funny lines on his face when he laughed. "You're a feisty little thing, Harriet," he said.

"In truth, I'd be disappointed in you if you flung your arms around me and called me Papa." He reached down to the floor then, into a leather briefcase, and pulled out some important-looking papers.

"You require proof," he said. "Very well. Here is proof. Here is my receipt of stewardship of the ship I came over on." He showed it to me. Sure enough, it said Richard Whitehead, and a lot of other fancy things in fancy writing. My father's ship. It was called the *Crusader*. And with that paper was a newspaper clipping from a London paper, telling of the sinking of the *Thomas Paine,* the ship my father was supposed to be lost at sea on.

"We were picked up by a German ship," he explained, "those of us who could keep afloat in the waters."

"They told us you were dead."

"I preferred it that way."

"Why?"

"Mrs. Whitehead and I were estranged. She wanted a divorce but knew she would be ostracized in her world for it. It was my way of giving her her freedom to run things herself."

"Richard ran them."

"But as I understood it, she was boss."

"Yes. How many years ago was that?" I asked.

He knew he had to answer me. He was, in effect, "on trial" here.

He said something that shocked me then. "How old is Violet?"

I couldn't answer for a minute. My brain couldn't take it all in. He couldn't be about to say what I thought. It would be too much like a novel. Such things didn't happen in real life, did they?

Margaret had once told me that truth was stranger than fiction.

"Three years older than I am," I told him.

"Then it was about fourteen years ago," he said. "Which brings us to the reason Mrs. Whitehead and I were estranged. Violet."

He cleared his throat. "I fathered her, Harriet. Forgive me. I'm afraid I'm an awful reprobate. Violet's mother was a negro here on the plantation who has since died. Mrs. Whitehead ignored that, as all wives of plantation owners do. But it was always there, between us. I couldn't forgive myself, so I decided to go to England to give the both of us time away from each other. That was when you were born, three years after Violet. I really learned my lesson in England, didn't I?"

I said nothing. Is that what I was? A lesson not learned?

He went on. "I knew the plantation needed tending, so I came home. Richard was already at Hampden-Sydney, intent on being a minister. And something strange happened. They all took to you. You were a fine little thing, all smiles and bright eyes and friendliness. Mrs. Whitehead fell in love with you in spite of herself. She was a good woman. I left you here and went back on the *Thomas Paine*. It sank."

"And you let us think you were dead," I said.

"Yes."

My head was spinning. I had to sit down. This family is going to kill me yet, I decided. I wish I could get on a ship and run away to England.

My uncle, father, or whatever he was, was looking at me. "I'm sorry for what all this has done to you, Harriet, but let me say I've never been so pleased about anything as finding you and how you turned out. I've heard stories about what happened around here and what you've been through, child, and, truth to tell, I don't know if I could come through it as well as you did."

"I love Violet," I said. "She's my best friend. And now I find out she's my half sister."

"Well, then we must bring her in here and tell her," he said.

I shook my head. "No. First you must tell me who my mother was."

He sighed. "Your mother disappeared on me two years after you were born. I tell you this carefully. Your mother was a beautiful and talented woman who belonged to a group of actresses and writers, men and women who were changing the face of literature and the role of women in England. Mary Lamb, and her brother, Charles Lamb, belonged to this group. They were a brother-sister writing team, part of a whole body of children's book writers in England. At that time, this group of writers was breaking new ground with children's books and were marked for their flamboyant ideas. Your mother was as liberal and flamboyant as the best of them. She put no restrictions on herself and everybody loved her. After you were born, I wanted to marry her, but she didn't want to marry. She wanted to be free. The group would have claimed you if I hadn't brought you here.

"I didn't even want them to know where you were. I only know I wanted you to grow up to be American. Catharine accepted you. She wanted you to be an out and out American. And this is why Richard raised you as he did."

"I hated Richard."

He withdrew another piece of paper from his portfolio. "I'm going to read this to you," he said. "It's a letter to me from Richard, after he was appointed pastor here and more or less took over the family. Sit quietly now and listen."

I sat quietly and he read.

Dear Father: Still being in a state of grace inside my heart from receiving the pastorship of Saint John's, I approach your request with the highest degree of open-mindedness. First, I wish to thank you for the trust you have invested in me and promise you that I will always honor Mother's wishes, and, in the case of disciplining a slave, which is definitely a man's work, I will work around her as delicately as I can without seeming to go in the face of those wishes.

Second, as to the girls. Margaret is a treasure and I can handle her with no problems at all. Violet has her place in the household and she knows what it is. It is never discussed that she is part of the family, but she is treated with decorum and a certain amount of respect. As for Harriet, I understand what you require in her upbringing and why. Her mother's flamboyant background needs reining in, and since this is in keeping with my beliefs as a minister, I shall see that she is trained this way. My God is a stern God, a punishing God, and will stand for no willy-nilly excuses, nor will I. She will have her chores, her schedule, her prayer times as well as study time. When I am finished, she will be as true an American woman as the Puritans at Plymouth. All vestiges of English nonsense will be gone from her.

I do think, however, that once she reaches a certain age, she should start to correspond with you, to soften some of the sharp edges. What I lack in the liberal arts of her education, she will receive from the tutor I hire, who will likely be my wife, Pleasant, and in later life from you. God bless you.

Your son, Richard

He smiled. "I hope, in time, you will be able to forgive Richard," he said quietly. "If you hate him for the way he raised you, you might as well hate me. It was by my orders."

I lowered my head. "He was good at what you wanted him to do," I said. "And at the end there, in the cotton field, I saw the real Richard, right before he died. He set the cotton afire to save my life."

He smiled. "As he should have."

There was silence for a while. It was getting on to dark. Somewhere in the house a clock chimed.

"Did my mother ever try to get me back?" I asked.

"Yes. But I was always able to prove her an unfit mother. After you were born, she left me. I never knew where she was. Or with whom."

Somebody knocked on the door of the office and he said, "Come in." It was Connie, who announced that she'd put supper on the table in the dining room.

He said thank you, and I simply did not know what to do.

"Shall we fetch Violet?" I asked.

"No," he said. "We'll have one meal alone, and then I'll talk to Violet. Alone, if it's all right with you."

"Yessir," I said.

We started in to the dining room and he asked me if I went to school and I told him about Pleasant and he said he'd see about a school for me. And he pulled out my chair when we sat down and I looked at him and said, "I don't know what I'm supposed to call you."

He smiled. "Many people along the way have puzzled over that. You can call me Father, or Papa, or Pa. I kind of like Papa. In England that's what the girls call their fathers. But take your time and get comfortable with it."

The soup came first, and it was good. And by the time it was finished, I had the courage to ask him a favor.

"So what are we going to do with the map, then?"

"Well, I think the proper thing is for me to bring it to the authorities. I'll tell them you found it. That you and the others were playing about as children do and found Nat Turner's cave."

I hesitated, then spoke. "Can I go with you?"

He looked at me. "In heaven's name, why would you want to do such a thing?"

"I want to see Nat Turner," I said.

His very expressive eyebrows raised up and he looked startled, but just for a second, then he had himself composed. And I thought, *I must learn how to do that.* And then I said, solemnly, "The only person Nat Turner killed, himself, was Margaret. I want to ask him why. Please. I have to know why."

Connie came in then and served the meat and potatoes and vegetables. I waited until she left.

Then I spoke again. "I know that he liked Margaret. I want to be sure he didn't let her suffer."

He was cutting his meat. "You can't let it be?"

"No, sir."

He buttered a roll. He said nothing for a moment. I said, "Please, Papa?"

He continued buttering the roll. I saw him bite his lower lip. That roll sure got a lot of butter on it. Finally he put it down on the plate and looked at me. "All right, daughter," he said.

Twenty-Six

"It's like something from a fairy tale," I told Violet, "us finding we're sisters."

I'd read her enough books in the past for her to know about fairy tales. We were in my room, where I was helping her into one of Margaret's dresses. Mine were too small for her, and she didn't seem to mind wearing Margaret's.

"I want you to dress according to your station in life," Papa had told her when they'd had their private talk in his office. "And no more servant's work. I'm going to get a tutor for both you and Harriet. I don't think she's ready to go to school yet and expose herself on a daily basis to the stares and questions and, yes, even the giggles of class-mates. So we'll keep on with tutoring for a while."

"It'll remind me of Pleasant," I told him.

"Everything will remind you of everyone for a long while," he explained quietly. "And if you can't climb up and out of those memories, we'll move. Get another plan-tation. There are plenty of them in Virginia, Harriet."

Violet looked scared. "I don't know how to do this," she said, adjusting the flower print dress. "All I've ever been is a slave."

"You haven't been that," I told her. "You've been my companion, practically my sister, anyway."

"But they *gave* me to you when I was just five."

"Yes. As a playmate."

"As someone to fetch for you. And carry. But I never ate with the family. And all Richard ever did was threaten and scold."

"That's all he ever did to me, too, Violet."

She looked beautiful in the pale green and yellow dress. I almost wished I had skin like hers. She stopped talking now to gaze into some middle distance while I was buttoning up the back of the dress. "What do you suppose Richard would do if he were alive today? And knew the truth about me?"

I stopped buttoning and thought a moment. "Richard did know. He knew all the terrible secrets about this family."

"You mean, when he started you writing to 'Uncle Andrew' he knew he was your father? And mine?"

"Yes. I believe he started the whole thing rolling. And watched it," I said, "waiting to see what would happen. Richard apparently did have a rich sense of humor. And if he hadn't been killed, you and I never would have met Papa."

"So," she said almost reverently. "It's a good thing, then, that he's been killed?"

"No," I said quickly. And for a moment both of us were wrapped in a terrible silence. And I knew it would take years, not minutes, for us to figure it all out.

For one thing, I knew I was going to have to start forgiving. Or at least understanding. First Richard, and then Nat Turner, and then my own mother and father, and then God.

Can one forgive God? Does He ever get the blame for anything? Richard would make me kneel an hour on the stones in the drive in back for even thinking such a thing.

"Forgive yourself," he would say. "You are to blame."

Was I? I know that some people went through all their life never forgiving themselves, but I did not want to do that.

"Can I go with you to visit Nat?" Violet was asking as we went downstairs.

"No," I said. "Oh, don't look so put out. I'm not being mean. I just think Nat won't talk if I'm not alone. Papa wanted to go in with me, too, but even he promised to stay outside the cell and give me my privacy. Isn't that decent of him, Violet?"

She agreed that it was. "I think he's going to spoil you," she said.

"I don't know what that would mean. People used to say Margaret was spoiled."

"Well, she was."

"Are you going to have a difficult time now? I mean, with all the servants?"

"They'll tease me, I suspect. Especially Owen. I'll have to get used to it."

"Did Papa tell you who your mama was?"

"No. He said someday. Someday when things are settled and the mood is right, he would tell me. He said she isn't living anymore."

More secrets, I thought, but I said nothing. Perhaps Papa was right. Enough had been said for now.

Owen brought the gilt and cherrywood brougham, pulled by two thoroughbred horses, up in front of the house and we got in.

Violet was coming along for the ride, for her own protection. The other servants hadn't been told about her new station in life yet. Papa would tell them when we got home. He didn't want any ruckus or teasing of her when they saw her in those clothes.

The November morning was true to its word, cold to the bones, dismal and gray. It looked like rain. Owen drove.

First there was the business with the map that had to be dispatched. Papa, a man to be reckoned with just on sight, was ushered into the office of the sheriff. He went in alone to deliver the map and give his story.

He was introduced, all around, and when the door opened and he came out, he was with several important-looking men who looked over at us and smiled. Papa gestured that we should come over, so we did. Violet and I gave our little curtsies and accepted their condolences for our losses.

"That brother of yours, the reverend, is a big loss to the community," the sheriff said.

"And we're so glad an adult is going to be in charge of the plantation. We were worried about Harriet, there all by herself, handling it alone."

"I'm proud of her," Papa said. "She did as good as Mother Whitehead would have done."

I basked in the praise.

"Brave girl you were, Harriet, running off like that to warn the Jacobses. If you hadn't, there's no telling what all would have gone on and who all would have been killed," the sheriff told me.

"Can she visit with Nat Turner?" he said in disbelief to Papa's request. "Don't know why anyone would want to. But if it helps her reason things out, of course she can. We'll just leave the door to where the cells are open. Thank you for the map, Mr. Whitehead. I'm sure it's already a historic document."

The room where the cells were was small and dank, with no windows. It was cold, a preserved coldness, like it had been held over from last year. *It's like a springhouse,* I thought. There were two cells. They said that Hark, Nat Turner's lieutenant, was in the other cell. I couldn't see him and didn't try.

The first thing I heard was the clanging of chains as Turner stood up when I presented myself. He was in leg irons and his hands were manacled, too.

It smelled in here. A smell of rotting flowers, or death, or dead animals.

He'd been here about two weeks.

I could see that his bed was a pine board. That he wore rags that barely resembled a shirt and breeches, that his feet were bare. The dank walls dripped with a wetness. The walls were crying. For him? For us?

But he was still Nat Turner, the preacher. He still thought that only he had the answers to the sins of mankind.

"Ah," he said, "the little girl of the map."

I said nothing. There was something I had to clear up with him right now.

"Hello, Nat. I won't ask you how you are. I can see. I've come to see you. On two counts. I have to ask you a favor."

"Me?" He laughed and held up his manacled hands. "Anything I can do for you, child. You want my blessing?"

"Nat, don't jest. I want a promise from you."

"I'm only gonna be around a couple more hours."

"Nat, please don't tell any of them that I had anything to do with the map."

"The map? Long gone," he said. "Lost."

"It isn't. It's been recovered and turned over to the magistrate. My name's been taken off it. That's what I'm asking you, don't you see? Please don't tell anybody I gave it to you."

"Lost," he said again. "My map is lost. If they have one, it's an imitation."

Well, if he wanted to think that, then let him think it, I decided. It was better that way.

"But I got it all in my head. You want to hear it?" And he started to recite. Like a prayer. "Travis," he said, "Salathul Francis, then Reese, then the Turner place, then Bryants, then Whitehead, then Porter, then Nathaniel Francis, then Harris, then Doyle, then Barrow, then Captain Newit Hams, then Waller, then Williams, then Vaughan. Did I forget anybody? I must have. Oh yes, Jacobs."

He gave a big sigh. "I saw you. I saw you running through the woods. You were running through the woods like you were being chased by the devil himself. Toward the Jacobs place. At first I wanted to go after you. But then I said no, let her go. Because, of a sudden, my spirit was low, and I felt a terrible grief. And I wondered if that's how God feels when He has to kill so many in a great tragedy. You see, I felt like God that day. But never once since. No, never."

"I need to ask you one more thing."

"Ask."

"Is it true that my sister, Margaret, is the only person killed by your hands?"

He scowled. "Beautiful, sassy Margaret," he said. "She never did know not to tease a man."

"Is it true?" I pushed.

"True as you're standing there."

"Why?"

"Why did I kill her? Or why is she the only one?"

"Anything you want to tell me."

He grimaced. "I killed her because of all the times she sassed me. All the times she bent over and showed me her bosoms. All the times she made me want her. And after I killed her, I couldn't bring myself to kill another. She was perfection. Nobody could come up to her as prey."

"Did she suffer? Did you make her suffer?"

He shook his head no. "It was clean and swift. Her beautiful blond hair soaked up the blood. But she didn't suffer. I promise you that."

He was lying. Even here. Even now. Now I had to burn her dresses and cloaks and shoes and everything. I couldn't give them, in good conscience, to Violet. I couldn't let Violet have her room with honest goodwill.

"Do you want to stay around and see me hanged?" Nat asked.

"No," I said. No. In years to come, everyone will know about Nat Turner. He will be famous. Remembered as two people: one who could preach and one who could kill.

"No, thank you," I said. I would remember him always as the man who killed everyone I loved. And those I still had to learn to love. I didn't need to see him hanged.

I left him there. In that room that was as cold as a springhouse, where the walls wept tears and it smelled of death.

Within six months my new father had sold our plantation and moved us, and all the animals and help, to another one on the other side of Jerusalem, which he called

"Harriet's Hope," because when Violet and I weren't studying under our new tutor, Papa let me have a hand in running it. And a say.

He wanted me to be myself again, he said, to forget the horrors. This new place is so lovely, there are days I think I can. And then there are the days I know I never will.

About Nat Turner

Nat Turner once talked about his mother's mother: "She was a girl of the Coromantee tribe from the Gold Coast of Africa, just thirteen years old when she was brought in chains to Yorktown, Virginia, aboard a schooner out of Newport, Rhode Island.

"She was sold in the harborside of Hampton, to Alpheus Turner, who was the father to Samuel Turner."

Nat Turner, himself, was born in 1800. At first Samuel Turner's brother, Benjamin, was his master, but when Benjamin died, he was given to Samuel. His next master was Thomas Moore, and then he went to Joseph Travis.

Nat Turner could not account for his ability to read and write. He was not only extremely intelligent but mechanically able and very influenced by religion in his life, a trait he attributed to his grandmother.

By the time he was twenty, Nat Turner considered himself a minister, though he was never officially ordained by anybody.

He described his "ordination" this way: "As I was praying one day at my plough, the spirit spoke to me. Which fully confirmed for me the impression that I was ordained for some great purpose in the hands of the Almighty."

There is no doubt that Turner considered himself a preacher. He spoke about "hearing a loud voice in the heavens and the Spirit instantly spoke to me."

All during his time of slavery, from birth in 1800 to his revolt in 1831, Nat Turner never gave any trouble to any of his masters or any of the people he was hired out to, like the Whiteheads. Even when he preached behind the vegetable stands in town or did baptisms in the nearby ponds, he did not agitate the crowds or cause a breaking of the peace.

So nobody, not even scholars in this day, can explain Turner's motives. Was it for liberty? For justice? For personal gain? How could any black man of Turner's obvious intelligence think he might organize an army (some say he had sixty men with him), destroy plantations, kill the people on them (white and black), capture a town (Jerusalem), and set up shop as an entity of his own without being captured?

All Turner knew was that this was his moment. That "the Spirit" told him to do it. Was he mad? One would think so. But then, how could he appear so polite and talented and agreeable to everyone in the months and years before?

It is worth pondering. At any rate, he was caught, he came to trial, and he was hanged on November 11, 1831. In today's world he is still not understood. The best historians cannot figure him out. Was he a criminal or a misunderstood holy man? Like others of his type, whose lives splash across the tabloids, perhaps we shall never know.

Author's Note

One of the first things I was asked when I told a group of teachers I was doing a book on Nat Turner was "Are you going to make him a hero?"

A hero? How can you make a hero out of a man who was responsible for the killing of fifty-seven people? And then I realized that she was asking about my "treatment," my "viewpoint," of Nat Turner. Would I consider him a victim? Or just a plain old killer?

What I have tried to do with this book is not impose my opinion on him at all, because, after all, it is said that he is our history's most misunderstood figure.

That I can agree with. And, since I finished writing the book with no handle on the motives or character of

Turner, I presume that is how I left him. Misunderstood in the sense that I certainly did not understand him. But he makes a darned good story.

When I first got the idea for *The Letter Writer*, Nat Turner was light-years away. If someone had told me I would someday write about him, I would have scoffed at the idea. The whole concept of his story was too overwhelming.

Important writers had fought, argued, and differed for years about how he should be viewed in our history. Did I dare put my two cents in?

All I wanted to do with this book was write a story about a young girl who was a "letter writer" for an elderly woman who was blind. That's the only piece of the puzzle I had when developing the plot. Who she was, where she lived, what century she lived in, I had no idea. But her role, somehow, must be critical to her well-being and her position important enough to those around her so that her actions might somehow save their lives.

That's all I had, but more than I usually have to start out with.

Then I must figure out the where and the when of it.

You have to be living under a rock these days not to know that young adult novels are getting sharper and more on the edge and, yes, riskier. Today's kids want more, so I decided to take the risk and put my girl (already named Harriet) against a backdrop so terrible for her time that Frankenstein would look like the Three Little Pigs.

The Nat Turner rebellion.

I found her a place in the Whitehead home. And then, while doing research, I came across an incident in which a fourteen-year-old girl is seen by Turner running through the woods in bare feet, hysterical and crying, running northward for help.

That was my Harriet, I told myself. I was on the right track.

And so it began.

I do not pretend, offering a book like this, to be as knowledgeable as the adult prizewinning authors who wrote about the Turner rebellion. I do not pretend to have any answers about it, any special information. Someday, perhaps, someone will.

I do not offer academic viewpoints or racial bias. I do not intend to foster arguments. My Harriet wrote her letters, as she was told, and when the time came, saved her world.

I simply offer that. A good read.

Bibliography

THE BOOKS I found most helpful for the time period of my novel are listed below, with many thanks to the authors who so painstakingly did the original work.

Berlin, Ira. *Many Thousands Gone: The First Two Centuries of Slavery in North America*. Cambridge, MA: The Belknap Press of Harvard University Press, 1998.

Betts, Edwin Morris, ed. *Thomas Jefferson's Farm Book*. Monticello, VA: Thomas Jefferson Memorial Foundation, 1999.

Franklin, John Hope, and Loren Schweninger. *Runaway Slaves: Rebels on the Plantation*. New York: Oxford University Press, 1999.

Greenberg, Kenneth, ed. *Nat Turner: A Slave Rebellion in History and Memory.* New York: Oxford University Press, 2003.

Mellon, James, ed. *Bullwhip Days: The Slaves Remember.* New York: Avon Books, 1988.

Styron, William. *The Confessions of Nat Turner.* New York: Vintage Books, 1967.